WHERE THE
RIVER
BIRCHES
BECKON

WHERE THE RIVER BIRCHES BECKON

FRED SCHLOEMER

BUTLER BOOKS

Designed by Eric Butler
Cover design by Scott Stortz

ISBN 978-1-941953-27-3

Printed in the United States of America
First printing March 2016

Published by
Butler Books
P.O. Box 7311
Louisville, KY 40257
phone: (502) 897-9393
fax: (502) 897-9797
www.butlerbooks.com

For my husband and best friend, Ernie Schnell, and in loving memory of all the brave runaway slaves and Underground Railroad operators who risked everything to combat slavery in an age when it was both unlawful and very dangerous to do so.

ACKNOWLEDGMENTS

First and foremost, I want to thank my editor, creative advisor, and friend, Susan Lindsey, owner of Savvy Communication, LLC, who is herself an accomplished writer, for her invaluable help with this project. This is the third book Susan has edited for me, and the last two won major awards, thanks largely, I believe, to her expert guidance and support. Susan not only proofreads and corrects grammar, punctuation, and spelling, but becomes a true partner in the writing process. In many ways I feel this latest collaboration is our best, because the story has been in my mind and heart for so long, that seeing it come to fruition through her help is very moving for me.

I also want to thank my lifelong friend, Richard Rosenbaum, and his lovely wife, Janet, for providing me with historical documents and photographs from the Market Street business district of Louisville in the 1800s. These materials helped me depict the town at that time in an authentic way.

Finally, my thanks also go to another long term friend and colleague, David Williams, a prolific writer, artist, activist, and curator of the Williams-Nichols Institute at the University of Louisville library, for additional proofreading and creative input.

AUTHOR'S NOTE

Slavery was an abomination. One might argue that the scourge it inflicted on our nation continues to this day in the racism, intolerance, and even violence we see reported in our daily news. Sadly, discrimination is still very much a part of American life, despite whatever progress we might have made toward greater equality.

As a result, I want to note that the presence in this story of African American characters who appear contented with their lot is not intended as a defense of slavery. I believe most, if not all, people yearn to be free, and throughout our history, countless slaves risked and lost their lives striving for freedom. I believe that anyone who had slaves in the first place was, by default, abusing those who were enslaved, no matter how contented they might have *seemed* to be. (After all, expressing discontent was not an option for most slaves).

However, our history also includes stories of slave owners and slaves who had strong emotional bonds, and who continued living together in interracial households even after slavery ended. Presumably, some good feelings held those people together.

Hopefully, the closing of the following tale explains exactly why these particular African American characters were so contented, despite living and working on a plantation in the era of slavery. Until you, the reader, reach that explanation, please know that this author is in no way rationalizing the institution of slavery by depicting several happy slaves in this fictional story.

—Fred Schloemer

WHERE THE RIVER BIRCHES BECKON

CHAPTER 1

Sarah woke as she had every other morning of her riverboat journey—puzzled at first about where she was, then smiling as she recognized the soothing sound of the paddle wheels turning. The foaming water cascading through the wooden paddles made a sibilant whisper that nearly lulled her back to sleep—until she remembered that this was the day she would reach Louisville.

Rising from her narrow bed in a second-deck cabin of the *Eclipse*, she stretched and stifled an unladylike yawn. Peering into a small mirror mounted on the wall, she brushed out and arranged her hair. Gazing at the face looking back at her, she wondered for the hundredth time since leaving Pittsburgh days earlier what the master of River Hill Hall might think of her, his new employee.

She hoped her high, clear brow and sharp, intelligent eyes might make a favorable impression. Or that her sincere oval face and small, shy smile might mitigate her plainness. She knew that she was no beauty and would never marry. Her father had told her so on his deathbed two months before.

"Rely on your brains, not beauty, my girl," he had said with a sigh, struggling for breath as his consumption worsened. "Your mother—God rest her soul—and I have loved you dearly, but I fear there'll be little romance in your life. No matter, you're very capable and shall make your way somehow. If only I'd been able to leave you a little something."

Days later, he fell still and died within hours. When he passed, she sat at his bedside, holding his hand until it grew cold. Getting up at last, she caught a glimpse of her reflection in a darkened windowpane and realized that it was true. She *was* plain—intelligent-looking too, perhaps—but still plain, and she could hardly imagine a worse fate for an unmarried woman in 1860. This world could be a harsh place for women who were not rich or attached to men; they were often destined for lives of service and even penury. In recognizing this inescapable truth, she had never felt more alone or vulnerable.

However, her father had also been right about her being very capable, and she soon took steps to prove it. She took stock of herself and her situation, and realized she wasn't without skills or resources. Since completing finishing school when she was eighteen, she had served as a secretary and assistant to her father, who was a scholar and figure of some prominence in local academic circles. He was also a demanding man of letters who expected nothing less than perfection from her, and she had risen to his every challenge.

When her mother and later her father became ill, she had spent a year nursing them at home. After their deaths, she found herself a smart, hardworking, but decidedly disadvantaged young lady of twenty-two. It was time to go to work in the outside world and soon.

Scanning the newspapers, she found several advertisements for posts as tutors, governesses, or nannies in wealthy homes. In an unexpected stroke of luck, the first one she wrote to replied within weeks, offering her a position as governess to a six-year-old boy. The letter writer, Squire Benjamin Booth of Louisville, Kentucky, described the boy as "grievously impaired since the demise of his mother in a recent carriage accident."

She hadn't been sure what to make of the description, but assumed the child must be in some kind of shock and needed special care. She wasn't put off in the least. In addition, Squire Booth had included money for her passage on a riverboat. She had liked his strong, elegant cursive and the rich, faintly tobacco-scented vellum paper, so she wrote him again, accepting the post.

That had been two weeks ago, and now she found herself nearing the time when she would finally meet the benevolent squire and his mysterious charge, presumably a son or other relation. She was a little daunted now that the hour was at hand. Still, she squared her shoulders and set her jaw, resolving to face whatever lay ahead with the resilience and fortitude her parents had instilled in her.

She had to admit that she was eager to leave the cramped boat that had been her home for the last several days. At first, the journey had seemed an exciting adventure, with so many new people and sights to see that her head swam. She had never been far from her parents' small urban rooms except to go to the neighborhood school, library, and local merchants, or the occasional concert or play.

Now she was surrounded by lush newly green spring fields on either side of the muddy river. It had still been cold and gray in Pittsburgh when she departed. On the boat, fashionably dressed women fanned themselves in the afternoon heat. Dandies sported Panama hats, tailored waistcoats, and tight butternut breeches. Sweating stevedores loaded or unloaded huge pallets of goods on the lower decks of the steamer whenever they docked.

She found one other new sight deeply unsettling—the frightened, scantily clad Negro slaves whom they had picked up when the boat crossed into Kentucky. The men were shackled at the ankles and chained to benches on the first deck. She found the sight heartbreaking. In addition to his post as a small private college professor, her father had also been an abolitionist, and she had often attended meetings with him where passionate speakers denounced slavery. Now she was confronted with its existence right under her nose. The ugliness of it frightened and appalled her.

It had never occurred to her that she would encounter slavery working in Louisville. She had read *Uncle Tom's Cabin*, which was set in Kentucky, and realized she should have expected as much. However, she had taken this post in near desperation, and it hadn't crossed her mind at the time. How would she handle it if her new employer treated his slaves harshly, starving or beating them? Could she, a female employee, stand up to the master of the house and confront him? How would she do it? What would she say?

It was too much for her strained nerves to process. These ethical questions, the cramped quarters, and the constant commotion on the boat, tried her patience to the point that she sometimes imagined jumping overboard to escape it all. Yet, that wasn't in her nature. She prided herself on being a survivor.

The fare the squire had sent her was generous, enough to save her from a long, grueling coach ride, but not enough to afford a stateroom on the boat. She had been satisfied with her tiny cabin, considering that steerage passengers slept on chairs or pallets on the decks. She dressed and went to the washstand where she doused her face with water and brushed her garments.

Looking down at the cheap second hand traveling suit her landlady had given her, she thought it had held up well, especially considering how long she had been wearing it. She wished it was a bit finer to make a more favorable first impression on her new employer, but no use in lamenting that. Beggars can't be choosers, she reminded herself. It would have to be good enough.

The boat whistle struck a long strident blast, signaling they were approaching a stopover, and the engines slowed. Finished with her grooming, Sarah hurried out to the deck and leaned over the rail. She peered downstream and saw a large creek flowing into the Ohio on the south side of the river. Numerous flatboats and skiffs crowded the river. To the west of the creek, on a small promontory, perched a sturdy stone cottage with a cedar shake roof; it was surrounded by several lean-tos and tents. A large sign read, "Harrod's Tavern est. 1811, Strong Spirits and Soft Beds for Suffering Sojourners."

Sarah smiled at the grandiose language but saw from the large assembly milling about the grounds that it must be working. Dozens of patrons mingled there, mainly unkempt boatmen in buckskins. They sported scraggly beards and long, greasy hair, and some of them stumbled about in various degrees of drunkenness, despite the early hour. She resolved to spend the layover on the boat. She would eat the apples and cheese she had stashed in her valise rather than go to the tavern for fresh food.

As the boat slowly approached the dock and lowered its gangplank, she was doubly glad of her decision, for it soon became apparent that the slaves were disembarking. They were turned over to the custody of a burly, hard-looking man who brandished a whip and bellowed curses.

"Get those shiftless bastards over here now before they try to take off! Not that they'd get very far in the state they're in. I got my dogs, and they's hungry for some *dark meat*."

He laughed at his own joke, and Sarah looked around to see if anyone else was repulsed by the man's behavior. Most of the other passengers were gossiping among themselves and totally unaware of the man. However, she eventually spied a tall, scholarly looking young man wearing spectacles and a fine linen suit; he seemed to be as disturbed as she was, if not more so.

Emboldened in a way that wasn't usual for her, she strode up to him and offered him her hand. "Sarah Brinley. Please pardon my directness, but do I detect that you may feel as disgusted as I am by this brute down on the riverbank?"

The young man shook her hand and smiled sadly. "Samuel Isaacs, and yes, I believe I am. I'm not from around these parts, though my family live here now, so I've never encountered this particular brand of barbarism firsthand. It truly is quite gruesome, isn't it?"

Sarah warmed to him right away. "Indeed, it is."

She glanced back down to the shore and saw that the slaves had been unloaded from the boat, and crowded into a buckboard by the tavern. They huddled there with panic on their faces, shivering and eyeing the drunken scene around them. The wagon slowly pulled away.

"How can human beings do this to one another?" she mused, half to herself and half to her companion. "Unless they're not really human beings, after all."

Samuel gave her an appraising look as if he were only now seeing her for the first time. He seemed to decide to trust her, new acquaintance though she might be. "I think you've arrived at the heart of the matter very quickly. Perhaps they're not human."

She heard a poignancy in his response that made her turn to look at him more closely. Yes, it was there, she saw now. He was deeply sad, though she didn't understand why. "Go on, please."

He drew a deep breath. "I came from Boston, where I was studying to become a rabbi. My family members are refugees from Russia, driven out by the Cossacks years ago. As soon as we arrived in the states, my parents enrolled me in Hebrew School up north where we had relatives, then they moved here. They started a profitable tannery, which my father ran until he died suddenly last month."

Sarah felt emboldened again and put a hand on his sleeve. "I'm so sorry."

Samuel looked down at her hand and seemed suddenly discomfited. "Oh, please, Miss Brinley, forgive me. I had no intention of becoming so maudlin. It's just that I've been summoned to take his place and forced to leave my studies."

They locked eyes, both smiling a bit self-consciously, and Sarah hoped that perhaps she had made a new friend. They noticed onlookers eyeing them, an unchaperoned woman and single man committing a definite breach of manners. They realized they'd probably best end their conversation. She offered her hand again, and he shook it once more.

"You haven't told me anything about yourself, so you must let me call on you once we arrive. Where will you be staying?" he asked.

"River Hill Hall, a plantation right on the river, southwest of Louisville."

A puzzled look crossed his face. "You'll be staying on a plantation? With a slaveholder?"

She blushed and stammered. "I know, I know. I can't imagine

what I was thinking, or rather, *not* thinking. I *had* to have employment—Father and Mother recently died—and it was the first thing that came up. I'll be caring for a sick boy."

"Well, that part sounds noble anyway, but I can't imagine how you'll get on there, feeling as you do about slavery."

He reached in his coat pocket, produced a card, and handed it to her. "Here's the address of my family's business. Come see me there . . . uh . . . if I can be of assistance in any way."

Now Sarah knew she had found a friend. "Thank you so much. I'll do that if need be."

Still blushing, she turned and hurried back to the wide deck at the stern of the boat. There she settled into a deck chair and tried to collect herself.

She clearly had her work cut out for her in more ways than one. Samuel had seen it instantly, even if she herself had failed to. Her mind was a jumble, going from being glad to have a job to wondering whether she was going to be able to do it at all.

She had been more deeply unsettled than she expected to be by her exposure to the shackled slaves and whip-brandishing slave trader. She had known of these things only as abstractions that she read about in books or periodicals or heard recounted by speakers at abolitionist meetings. Now they were right before her eyes, and they were no longer abstractions, but a dark, soul-wrenching reality. The experience left her stomach and mind reeling, and she questioned whether she would be able to work on any plantation, no matter how well the master might treat his slaves. The very institution of slavery was so monstrous to her now that she wished she could reverse the big boat and return to Pittsburgh.

The whistle shrieked again, and the big wheel began to turn, guiding the boat back into the river currents. She looked at the shore and saw the revelers by the tavern growing rowdier. She was glad to leave this place. It was only an outpost of Louisville, a town she had read about and believed to be a civilized, even refined place. However, the vicious slave trader and the unkempt, rowdy boatmen had left her nervous about what she might expect in Louisville—especially at River Hill Hall.

CHAPTER 2

The Louisville levee was approximately seven miles downriver from Harrod's Creek. With a strong wind at their back, the *Eclipse* made good time getting there. Stewards scurried about the decks and staterooms alerting passengers that they would dock within the hour. That was no problem for Sarah, who had only a single valise. More affluent passengers ordered their servants about, pushing them to gather their numerous trunks and hatboxes, and prepare to disembark.

Sarah began packing the few odds and ends left on her washstand—a comb, a brush, a small bottle of rosewater, and the simple cameo brooch her mother had left her, which she wore pinned over her heart, whenever she went out into the world. Once packed, she let her fingers wander across the worn leather surface of the case, remembering the day her parents had given it to her. They had saved every nickel and dime to pay for a year's tuition and board at a young women's finishing school—her "ticket to a better life," her father had called it. It was her eighteenth birthday, and they announced this portentous news to her over her favorite breakfast of popovers and jam, their faces beaming with pride.

Her father also presented her that morning with the used, though clearly well-made and once-costly valise. Her parents were so excited that she hadn't had the heart to tell them that she had no desire to go to finishing school to become a more refined lady.

However, she couldn't decline their gifts, so she had feigned excitement, much to their delight. She completed her year at the finishing school, surprised to find that she did consider it valuable, after all. As the only child of a dedicated academic, she had read widely and studied vigorously all of her life. However, she had had little training in matters of etiquette, ladies' attire, and comportment, all of which she received in spades at boarding school.

Admittedly, she had found some of the lessons odd to the point of absurdity. She had never been able to fully accept mandates such as "a woman must always address a man with eyes downcast and voice carefully modulated" and "never volunteer a serious opinion on any topic in conversations with men." She understood the origins of these ideas—the United States may have won independence from Great Britain long before, but American manners were still strongly influenced by the social dictates of the prudish British monarch, Queen Victoria. However, Sarah had filed away all of the pearls of wisdom dispensed at school as nuggets of information that might be useful someday. One of her father's favorite axioms had been that one never knew when knowledge gained might be knowledge used.

Now, preparing to leave her cabin, she let her hands linger a moment more on the warm leather surface of the old valise, and thought of her parents with love and longing. They had sacrificed so much for her, fully believing they were preparing her for a better life than theirs had been. Despite the financial situation they had left her in, she knew that they had indeed given her many gifts. The only problem was, she wasn't sure how to best use those gifts in the time to come. There were too many uncertainties about what she would encounter in the days ahead. With a wistful sigh, she gave the cabin one last glance to make sure she had everything, then went out on deck.

As the big boat neared its destination, Sarah stood at the rail, watching the city skyline come into focus, enjoying the wind in her hair and the mounting air of excitement all around her. A German immigrant family who had ridden in steerage outside her cabin joined her, chatting in their native tongue. The children jumped up and down, and clapped their hands as the city loomed nearer. She had to admit, she shared their anticipation, even if she didn't express it in the same way.

When the city had morphed from a distant view to clearly defined streets and buildings, she found it appealing for the most part. On both the Kentucky and Indiana riverbanks, numerous grand homes perched on manicured lawns dotted with huge shade trees and formal flower gardens. Closer to downtown Louisville, she spotted the Howard Shipyard in Jeffersonville, Indiana, where many of the boats plying America's rivers had been built. As they passed the busy plant, Sarah looked up at the wheelhouse of the *Eclipse* and saw a brass plaque reading "Howard Shipyard."

As the boat maneuvered into a berth on the wharf, she could see that the town itself appeared to be a pretty place, much cleaner and airier than Pittsburgh. Countless church steeples rose into the skyline. Beyond the levee, three- and even four-story business buildings and warehouses stretched as far as the eye could see, many with gleaming copper roofs and tall brick chimneys.

She had visited the library before leaving Pittsburgh, where she learned that Louisville was the tenth-largest city in the country and one of the fastest growing. It was home to numerous thriving businesses, including banks, breweries, distilleries, and meatpackers. It had several world-class hotels, most notably the Galt House, where Charles Dickens had stayed in 1842. He had described it as every bit as elegant as any hotel in Paris. However, a pall of coal and wood smoke, trapped by the walls of the surrounding river valley, hung over the city and blackened the walls of the older buildings.

The levee, like most levees in most river towns, was a muddy morass, seething with the planned pandemonium that commerce and shipping generate. Men drove horses, mules pulled wagons, and carts teemed everywhere, unloading goods from some of the docked boats and loading goods onto other boats. The noise was cacophonous: mules brayed, horses nickered, men cursed, and steamboat whistles blared.

The cries of street vendors added to the tumult. They wove their way among the wagons, carts, and scurrying pedestrians hawking their wares, everything from fruit to fried pies and patent medicines. After days stuck on a crowded boat, watching rural landscapes, Sarah found the vibrant urban scene an engaging sight. She liked Louisville immediately. She only hoped she would find life at River Hill Hall equally appealing.

Once the *Eclipse* docked and the gangplank was lowered, she joined the press of passengers filing off the boat. Back on land at last, she lifted her skirts to escape the mud of the levee, but her boots were another matter. They were soaked within seconds, and she could do nothing to prevent it.

She scanned the busy scene for some sign of anyone who

appeared to be looking for her. To her relief, a handsome young Negro man in livery stood by a buggy at the top of the levee, holding a hand-lettered placard that read, "Escorting Miss Brinley." Working her way through the crowd, she finally made it to him.

"I'm Miss Brinley. Thank you for meeting me."

"I'm Jesse," he replied. "Welcome, miss. Let me take that bag for you."

He handed her up into the buggy and strapped her valise into a rack on the back. Hopping in beside her, he clucked to the horse, and pulled into the busy traffic on River Road.

Everywhere Sarah looked, there was bustling activity. The stores lining the streets were all doing a brisk business, and Sarah took note of the ornate sculpted iron storefronts on many of the establishments. She had seen these new architectural features in Pittsburgh, but there were far fewer of them there.

"My, what a busy town," she said.

"Yes, miss," Jesse agreed. "Louisville is that indeed."

As he spoke, Sarah noticed that he spoke in a clear, melodious voice, free of any Southern drawl or the colloquial speech patterns of every other Negro she'd ever met.

"You have a lovely voice," she said, then felt perhaps she had been rude to comment on a personal trait.

"Thank you, miss. The squire says he wants all his people to be well spoken. He has us learn what he calls 'proper King's English' when we're little ones."

Sarah mulled over this information. She had always understood that it was deeply frowned upon, and even illegal, in some Southern states to educate Negroes beyond teaching them whatever work or trade they were expected to do.

"And who teaches you?" she asked.

A cloud passed across Jesse's face. "Well, it was the missus, until . . ."

"I'm sorry," Sarah said. "I didn't mean to bring up something painful."

He turned to her and managed a smile. "That's all right, miss. You couldn't have known."

They had worked their way up Second Street to Market Street. Jesse told her the street would take them southwest all the way to the plantation. However, as they prepared to turn onto Market Street, Sarah gasped and put a hand on Jesse's arm.

There at the corner of Second and Market Streets was a collection of pens. Men in waistcoats and top hats peered into them with intense scrutiny. Inside the pens, a dozen or more Negro men, women, and children, some naked or half-dressed, stood huddled together for comfort. Sarah couldn't keep the image of a zoo out of her mind, and she felt sudden nausea.

"Oh, my God," she whispered.

Jesse followed her gaze to the pens and frowned. "Yes, miss, Louisville has a busy slave trade."

He clucked to the horse again and it picked up its pace. Sarah realized he was trying to hurry her away from this upsetting scene and she was touched. She also realized she still had her hand on his arm, and that this was probably a serious breach of Southern manners. She snatched it away.

"I'm sorry, again. It's . . . it's just that I've never seen such a horrible thing. I'd heard about it, of course, but I don't think I fully believed something so dreadful could exist. Odd, I was just talking to Mr. Isaacs on the boat about this, how I'd handle living in a slave state, I mean."

Jesse's face lit up. "Would that be Mr. Samuel Isaacs?"

"Why, yes. It was."

"Well, the squire is waiting at his home to welcome him right now. He was close to old Mr. Isaacs. They played chess every Sunday and owned some racehorses together. It about killed him to lose the old gentleman, right on top of losing the missus, too."

Sarah was surprised once more. Today seemed full of all kinds of revelations. Somehow, she wouldn't have expected a man who held slaves to be friendly with Jews, whom she had understood were also generally oppressed in the South. It didn't fit into her assumptions about the kind of character it took to be a slave owner—a type that could deny the humanity of an entire race of people. Then she blushed as a guilty thought struck her. *Maybe I'm the prejudiced one.*

As they passed the business district, her attention was diverted to her surroundings. They were passing through a neighborhood of tidy row houses right on the street, with small, neatly trimmed gardens behind wrought iron fencing. The neighborhood had a distinctly European air to it, and Jesse explained that it was called Shippingport, and was occupied largely by French immigrants.

Her positive first impression of Louisville crystallized as they moved into yet another district that Jesse called Portland. There the townhouses gave way to larger homes sitting farther back from the street on wide, clipped lawns beneath towering shade trees. Many of the lawns had children playing on them, rolling hoops, tossing balls, or chasing each other in games of tag. Most of these children also had an adult Negro woman standing somewhere nearby, watching over them and tending to the occasional tumble or tussle.

Peering more closely, Sarah realized that the groups of children included both white and Negro children.

"Jesse, those children are playing *together*."

He looked puzzled. "And?"

"I thought the Negro children were the white families' slaves."

"They are, mostly, although there are more than a thousand free Negroes in Louisville. Still, why shouldn't the children play together?"

She realized that she had made another assumption. "Oh, never mind. It seems *Uncle Tom's Cabin* isn't a very reliable travel guide. I think I need to merely watch, listen, and learn for a while."

He smiled, and they lapsed into a companionable silence for the next few miles of their journey. Reflecting on Jesse's easy, accepting attitude, Sarah felt she had made another important friend.

Just as Jesse told her that they were almost to their destination, they came to a place in the road where a thick forest encroached on the thoroughfare, blotting out the cheerful sunlight. Vines covered the floor of the forest and crawled up the trunks of the trees. They wound all the way to the ends of the lower branches until they hung down over the roadway, like ghostly fingers trying to grasp at passersby. The temperature dropped several degrees in the heart of the thicket and Sarah found herself shivering. She wrapped her shawl closer around her shoulders and turned to Jesse with an anxious face.

"What *is* this place?" she asked and realized that she was whispering.

Jesse shifted in his seat and she sensed he was as uncomfortable as she was. "They call it the Whipping Woods," he said, whispering too.

"Because of the vines up there whipping in the breeze?" she asked.

He shook his head with a sad smile. "No, because of those," he said, pointing at a clearing on the north side of the road.

Sarah followed his pointed finger and saw several posts with irons hanging from them. Goosebumps rose on her neck and arms and her scalp tingled. "Is that . . ." she stopped in midsentence. She couldn't bring herself to voice the monstrous question.

"Yes," Jesse said. "None of the masters in these parts treat their folks badly, but there are bands of vigilantes who patrol the region and take matters into their own hands if they think any of the local slaves are getting to be what they call 'uppity.' Usually they just put a scare into them, a few lashes in a big public display to remind folks to keep their place. Sometimes they go too far though, and a man dies from a lashing. Right before Christmas, they killed one of the men from the Soames plantation we passed a ways back. He'd 'looked the wrong way' at a white woman in town."

Sarah had thought the chained slaves on the boat and the slave market in town were bad, but they paled in comparison to this newest horror. "How . . . how perfectly ghastly. Can't the local law enforcement officials control them?"

The tolerant look Jesse gave her in response let her know how naïve she'd been. "Oh, I see. They're complicit then."

Jesse didn't answer, but shook the reins over the horse's back to encourage him to move faster. As he did, a strong gust of wind came from nowhere and blew swirls of dust across the roadway. The moaning wind sounded to Sarah like spectral voices warning of bad things to come, and she shivered again.

Jesse seemed to intuit what she was thinking. "Some of the

field hands believe this place is haunted. They say the souls of those who died here hide among the trees waiting to wreak their revenge on anyone who comes through here. They won't pass through it at night and sometimes not even in the day unless they're in a big group of people. I don't believe in such things, of course."

Sarah thought he was trying to reassure her, or perhaps himself, with this last comment. Fortunately, they were soon through the sinister thicket and golden sunlight greeted them again as they emerged from the darkness of the towering trees. Sarah tried to put the unpleasant experience out of her head, but found it harder to do than she would have liked.

The old saying about how bad luck comes in threes came to her mind. Her excitement at arriving in Louisville had now been marred by three events: shackled slaves being unloaded amidst drunken revelers at Harrod's Landing; the slave market in town; and now this, the Whipping Woods, not far from her where she would be living and working soon. She hoped these three events were simply unfortunate coincidences and not a portent of things to come at the hall. However, having experienced so much sadness and loss in the previous year, she had a hard time shaking her fears.

CHAPTER 3

By the time they arrived at River Hill Hall, the sun was beginning to set. All along their route, Sarah saw numerous farms situated on fertile, black bottomland. Many had fine brick or frame farmhouses with wide verandahs where people sat sipping tea or juleps. Nowhere, though, did Sarah see any houses that she would have described as "plantation homes"—no imposing Greek revival residences with grand columns and peacocks strutting about the grounds. Instead, most of the homes tended to be mere farmhouses. As they pulled into the drive that led to River Hill Hall, Sarah had to ask another question.

"Jesse, where are all the mansions?"

He threw her another quizzical look. "What mansions, miss?"

"Well, I thought plantations all had big mansions."

"Not that I know of, miss. Not around here, anyway. Most folks only build something big enough for their family and servants. I can't say that I've ever seen a mansion, except in town where all the *really* rich folks live."

Sarah smiled behind her hand, hearing him characterize slaveholders as not *really* rich. She had a hard time imagining anyone who could own hundreds of acres of land and dozens or more slaves—who were tremendously expensive—as not really rich.

She looked all around her as they made their way up a long tree-lined drive to the house. Everywhere she saw evidence of a well-managed estate. The four-board fences that enclosed the fields were all newly painted black. She could smell the fresh paint in the moist evening air. Spring crops had recently been planted, and small sprouts of green were starting to emerge. She saw cattle and horses grazing in distant fields. The sounds of an occasional steer lowing or horse neighing wafted on the soft evening breeze. These sights and sounds both charmed and soothed her.

Jesse followed her gaze at the surrounding fields. "Corn mostly, for livestock feed, and the bourbon distilleries south of town. Then, there'll be tobacco later. The squire's tobacco is some of the most prized in the state. He also breeds thoroughbreds and runs a profitable ferry down at the river. Boats and barges stop over to unload goods, and the crews buy box lunches from Momma Annie. All things considered, he does pretty well."

She nodded, taking it all in. By the time they reached the end of the drive, a wide circular turnaround in front of the house, the sun had dropped behind the horizon and only its fading rays lit the landscape. Lamps and candles already burned inside the house, and all the windows glowed with a rosy, welcoming warmth. She could still see well enough to establish that River Hill Hall was yet another basic farmhouse, although a large and impressive one, with beautifully proportioned, symmetrical lines.

Jesse told her that it had been built in 1800 of red brick that had been fired on the grounds by slaves. The style was Georgian, with tall white-trimmed windows and black shutters that contrasted smartly with them. A wide front porch and brick steps seemed to beckon visitors to enter and partake of the hospitality of a gracious house and its host. She began to feel a bit relieved.

Jesse hitched the horse to a post and handed her down from the buggy. Seeing that she was still a little unsteady on her feet after days on a boat, he held her elbow as she made her way up the front steps.

"I think I'm all right now," she said as they reached the porch. The door swung open, and a portly old Negro woman waved her in.

"Momma Annie, this is Miss Brinley," Jesse said.

The woman beamed and curtsied. "Yes'm, the young lady that's gonna teach our li'l boy. Welcome, miss. Young master's in town with his daddy now, but you'll meet him in the morning."

Hearing the Negro speech patterns she was used to, Sarah shot a glance at Jesse, who broke into a mischievous grin.

"Momma Annie rules the roost here, Miss Brinley. *Nobody*, even the squire, tells *her* how to talk."

"You mind your manners," Annie chided him. "You may be a grown man now, but you're still my grandchild and I can still take a switch to you if I've mind to."

Jesse laughed, and went to retrieve Sarah's bag before his grandmother could make good on her threat.

"Slip off them muddy shoes, miss, or you'll muck up my pretty floors. I'll fetch you some house slippers shortly."

Though not in the least offended, Sarah was surprised by the housekeeper's imperious tone with her. She decided that Annie must indeed "rule the roost" here and she did as she was told. Annie shepherded her into a front parlor that seemed to serve as a library, and settled her in a comfortable chair by a crackling wood fire.

"You must be plum wore out," she clucked over her. "Let me fetch you tea and some soup I got on the stove." She bustled out and left Sarah to survey her new surroundings.

As Jesse had stated, the hall was essentially a very fine farmhouse, rather than an elegant mansion. However, everywhere she looked she saw evidence of owners who had refined taste and plenty of money. Most notable was a large portrait over the mantel of a strikingly beautiful woman with a kind face and gentle smile. Sarah presumed the lady must be the deceased mistress. She felt a pang of sympathy for the family she was about to meet who had lost a woman so lovely and kind-looking. The portrait also gave her reason to glance down with a resigned sigh at her own comparatively shabby appearance. Her father had certainly been right that she was no beauty, but she could do nothing about it other than continue to strive to make herself as presentable as possible.

Scanning the rest of the room, she noted that the walls were papered in what was clearly an expensive covering, probably French, she surmised. She spotted scenes from various Greek myths—a nymph eluding an amorous Apollo; Narcissus gazing at his reflection in a pool; Icarus flying too close to the sun. The woodwork and substantial wainscoting were a light walnut, and the floors, wide oak planks burnished to a brilliant shine with plush oriental carpets on them. The furnishings were simple yet elegant in an understated way.

The house had none of the elaborate, heavy Victorian upholstery and cabinetry that were the current rage. Instead, it was furnished with rather plain, expertly crafted settees, secretaries, bookshelves and gaming tables in various hardwoods, mostly cherry, mahogany, and walnut. The overall effect was one of comfort combined with style, a pleasing balance of things that were pretty with things that were functional.

Sarah wondered who had designed and appointed these rooms so well. Was it the deceased wife and mother, the squire himself, or someone else? Somehow, she imagined the squire and his wife working together on them, and the thought brought a sudden sadness to her. How devastating it must be to lose one's wife and be left with a small child to rear alone.

The pocket doors into the room slid open with a faint whisper, and Annie reappeared, ushering in a small boy carrying a silver tray almost as big as he was. The tempting aroma of fresh rolls, mint tea, and a savory potage of some kind reached Sarah, and she felt intense hunger pangs. She remembered that she hadn't eaten anything since her breakfast of fruit and cheese on the boat. The ride here with Jesse had been so full of new sights as well as insights that it had never crossed her mind. Now that she smelled food, she was ravenous.

Annie watched her young liege with a mixture of pride and anxiety. "This here is Lije, my youngest grandchild. His momma passed in childbirth, so he feels more like my own son. He's eight years old and just started to serve in the house."

"Lije is short for Elijah," the boy explained. "How do you do, miss?" He flashed her a stellar, white smile. She noticed that he, like his older brother Jesse, had a pleasant voice and perfect diction. He managed to navigate his way through the room to a tea table at Sarah's side, where he deposited his tray to his grandmother's obvious relief, then gave them both another broad smile.

"Well done, Lije," Sarah said. "You're a quick learner."

"All my boys are," Annie said, beaming. "Now let's get some food in you."

"This smells wonderful. What is it?"

"Burgoo, miss, a stew of vegetables, pork, chicken, and game." She handed Sarah a big bowlful along with a hot buttered roll. "I made you some mint tea, too, to soothe your tummy, and put lots of honey in it."

Sarah dove into the meal with relish and found it all delicious. "This is wonderful, Momma Annie. May I have some more, please?"

"Why of course, miss. I'll be right back with that, and some slippers, too."

She bustled out of the room, shooing Lije before her. Sitting by the fire, watching the embers glow, with the warmth of the tea and stew beginning to relax her, Sarah found herself nodding off. By the time Annie came back with a second helping, she was sound asleep. Taking a knitted afghan from the settee, Annie arranged it on Sarah's lap, set a pair of slippers at her feet, then banked the fire.

The old woman looked down on her and muttered a quick prayer.

"Sweet Jesus, please give this young lady strength and heart. We need this one to stick around." With that, she snuffed out the candles and closed the parlor doors as she left.

CHAPTER 4

Sarah awoke with a start, wondering where she was. When she did recall, she felt a twinge of anxiety and confusion. What was she doing sleeping in the library? Soon, the evening's events came back to her, and she recalled that she had trailed off to sleep by a cheerful fire, full of Momma Annie's tasty burgoo. A huge grandfather clock in the corner struck four a.m., and she realized it wouldn't do to rouse anyone to get her to a proper bed at this time of the night. She might as well stay put, so she settled back in her chair and tried to return to sleep.

It was no use. She had too much on her mind and too much to look forward to in the days ahead. Soon she would be meeting the squire and her young student and presumably, many other new faces as well—other servants and workers on the plantation. Suddenly the naïveté of that thought struck her, as she remembered that all the help on the place were slaves, not servants, and she felt another quick stab of anxiety. How would she find it, working alongside people who were considered chattel, and how would the master relate to them?

As she mulled over all this, she heard the front door open and close again with a soft thud, and voices came to her from the hall outside the library door. She heard Annie welcoming someone in a soft, loving tone; a small child's shrill cry, no words, merely a sleepy, frustrated wail; and a man's resonant voice reassuring the child.

"Papa should never have kept you out so late, but you're home now, safe and sound."

"That's right, child. Annie's got your covers turned down and a nice fire in your grate. Come on up with me now, baby."

The male voice detained her. "One more thing, Annie. We have more *visitors* coming again soon. Did you finish the quilt?"

Sarah thought it odd that he emphasized the word *visitors*, and would be discussing quilts in the middle of the night with a sleepy child needing his bed.

"Yes, sir. Stitched the last of it up this evening."

"Well, good work, Annie, and fast. You know what to do next. Hang it as usual over the rails on the back verandah."

"I sure will, sir. Now, you let me get this child in bed right quick, or he'll be fussy all day tomorrow."

"Of course. I'll come along and help tuck him in."

Sarah thought it odd that the squire would have Annie hang a new quilt for visitors over the back porch railing. Maybe he wanted it aired out before she put it on the visitors' bed.

She also thought it noteworthy that there had been a clear reproachful tone in Annie's last comment to her master and that he had accepted it without dressing her down for being disrespectful. Clearly, Jesse had been right about Annie's authority. The interaction she'd overheard had a certain reassuring effect on her, though. The squire spoke with warmth and affection to his son and with appreciation, even respect, to Annie. Perhaps he was no Simon Legree from *Uncle Tom's Cabin*, after all.

She was also reassured that he had a kind, calm manner, at least with his child and servant—*slave*, rather, she reminded herself—

and that was a good thing. When she had first corresponded with him, she had liked his elegant writing style. Now she found that she also liked the deep baritone timbre and slight Southern drawl of his voice. It was very, very pleasant.

Considering all this, she found herself too keyed up to even think about going back to sleep. She threw off her cover, pulled on the slippers Annie had left for her, and went to stir the embers in the fireplace. Once a flame flickered, she took a couple of small logs from the copper bin beside the hearth and placed them on the embers. Soon she had a hot fire going, and she warmed her hands before it. Glancing about the room again, now basked in a rosy glow, she thought once more about how pretty and comfortable it was. All in all, her first few hours at River Hill Hall had been very encouraging.

Wide-awake at last, she took a candlestick from the mantel, lit it in the fire, and used it to light the other candles and oil lamps in the room. As the library came into clearer view, she went to peruse the many bookshelves lining the walls. There she learned more about her new boss's tastes and character, and perhaps those of his wife and father, as well.

The shelves contained a veritable treasure trove of books on all sorts of topics and from authors across the ages. There were ancient Greek and Roman philosophers, Homer, and all the great Greek plays, many of them in the original Greek; the complete works of Shakespeare, Marlowe, Swift, and Defoe; Baudelaire, Rabelais, and other French poets, dramatists, and satirists; tomes on agriculture, animal husbandry, and architecture; and everything the prolific Mr. Dickens had written so far.

As a lover of Dickens, she couldn't resist taking down one of his volumes and browsing through it. In the front pages of

A Christmas Carol, she found an inscription: "To Benjamin, with deepest gratitude for your hospitality when I visited your fair city last year and with highest regards for your young bride, Eleanor—a true lady and great beauty. Your humble servant, C. D. 1843."

Sarah felt another surge of compassion for the widowed squire and his motherless son. She was so engrossed in that feeling and her appreciation for the bounty of books all around her that she didn't hear the pocket doors slide open behind her.

"So, you're a reader, Miss Brinley. That's a good thing in a governess."

Startled, she almost dropped the book. She whirled to face the squire, a ruggedly attractive fortyish man with a tousled mane of prematurely gray hair. He was wearing an open-collared linen shirt and dusty black riding clothes and boots.

Having never had either a job or an employer before, she suddenly realized she didn't know what the expected greeting was. Did she curtsy as Annie had to her? Bow? Shake hands? She found herself frozen with a blush beginning to burn her face when he settled the matter for her.

"Pardon me for startling you," he said and came to shake her hand. As he did, she noticed the strength in his large, calloused palm, and she was struck by the raw, earthy energy he emanated. Though he was not a conventionally handsome man, his energy was infectious and she found him extremely charismatic.

"I saw the light under the door and wanted to inquire after your comfort. You must think us Southerners terribly uncivilized, making you spend your first night here in a chair." She thought she saw a little twinkle in his luminous brown eyes.

"Oh, not at all, sir. It was my fault for falling asleep here in the first place. I'd had a big bowl of Annie's burgoo, and I nodded off before I knew it."

He smiled again, then looked down at their hands, still joined in a handshake, and quickly withdrew his. Sarah thought he seemed a bit embarrassed. If so, he covered it with a small cough, and changed the subject.

"You had a good journey, I trust?"

"Oh, yes, thank you. I'd never been on a riverboat before and I found it enchanting . . . well, mostly anyway." She knew she could never mention her horror at the slaves on board. "I hate the dust and cramped quarters of coaches, so a riverboat ride was quite an unexpected luxury."

She stopped herself, seeing that he was scrutinizing her in a speculative way, his eyes narrowed slightly, and she wondered if she'd been too familiar with him. Would she ever figure out Southern ways, or would she be fired forthwith for transgressing their peculiar mores? He seemed to catch himself and apologized.

"I was trying to place your accent. I've been to Pittsburgh many times on business and have always found the people there to have a very pronounced, clipped way of speaking, which you have none of. I'm a bit of an aficionado of speech and language matters, you see."

"Ah, yes, Jesse told me," she said and immediately wondered once more if she was being too forward. He didn't appear to mind, though, so she forged on. "My father also loved language and insisted I take elocution from an early age. 'Nothing marks a lady like a refined speaking voice,' he always said."

The squire seemed to stifle a smile. "Well, you certainly have that. Tell me, what drove such a refined lady to leave home and venture so far for employment, and in service, at that?"

She thought perhaps he was mocking her a bit but felt she owed him a respectful answer nonetheless. Still, she found her voice shaking and had to fight back tears as she recounted the events of the previous year—losing her parents, one after the other, and waking up one day impoverished and orphaned. When she finished, she was relieved to see a compassionate look on his face.

"Well, then, we are fortunate to have found each other. We are in great need of your skills, Miss Brinley, and it appears you are in need of us a bit too, perhaps?" She found herself fighting tears again, although they were tears of relief this time.

"Why, yes, yes, indeed," she said, grateful for his chivalry, casting her misfortune in more positive terms.

He changed topic and asked, "Tell me, which of my friend Mr. Dickens's works are you familiar with, and do you have any favorites?"

"Oh, all of them, sir, so much so that it's hard to name a favorite. If pressed, I suppose I'd have to say *Oliver Twist*."

"An apt choice. Orphaned boy overcomes adversity and finds family and love. May our stories end as happily."

She wasn't sure how to take his last comment—it almost seemed flirtatious to her, although admittedly she had little experience of such things—so she assumed he was merely trying to be encouraging. He looked past her at the windows. "It appears we've talked the night away. Look, the sun is coming up."

She turned and saw that it was true. The tall casement windows all around the room were lit with a faint pink light, and on the horizon, she saw a fiery red sunrise spilling across the skies.

"Perhaps you'd like to go back to sleep? I can have Annie take you up to your rooms."

"Rooms? Plural?"

"Well, yes. They're quite modest, and on the third floor to boot. However, there's a sleeping room and a small anteroom with a nice fireplace where you can sit and read. Annie has made it quite nice with her quilts and throws. You see, we've never had a governess—haven't needed one, until . . ."

His face clouded, exactly as Jesse's had when he mentioned the plantation's deceased mistress, but he soon recovered and carried on. "So, to be frank, we haven't quite known how to prepare for you."

Sarah was both touched and a bit amused. "I've never been a governess either," she admitted with an embarrassed smile. "But I'm well read and curious about everything and eager to learn all that I don't know. I'm going to do my best to be the finest governess any child ever had."

He gave her that speculative look again. "I think you're going to be . . . just *fine*. Well, what is it to be? To sleep or to work? After some breakfast, that is."

"To work. After breakfast, that is."

"I'll turn you over to Annie, then, and she'll take good care of you. Now if you'll excuse me, I have some things I need to tend to." He took a step back, bowed his head, and left the room.

"Annie, Miss Brinley is hungry!" She heard him bellow as he slammed the massive front door behind him. For some reason, she found herself feeling out of breath and somewhat confused . . . but a little giddy, too.

CHAPTER 5

Sarah's education about Southern ways, and this particular plantation and its inhabitants, continued at breakneck speed. She learned that the squire had been honest when he confessed that they didn't know how to deal with her. She was an employee, so she was expected to be of service and to do what was asked or needed of her. Yet she was also a lady, and a well-bred and educated one at that. These traits were highly prized in the South, so she was always treated with complete deference.

Still, she was a Northerner, all of whom were slightly suspect as tensions between the states mounted. Except for the overseer, who managed the field workers, she knew that everyone else on the plantation was a slave. At times, she sensed that the squire wanted to invite her to have tea or dinner with him, but withheld because he wasn't sure it would be appropriate. On the other hand, every time they crossed paths as they went about their business during the day, he was invariably pleasant, respectful, and, she sensed, glad to see her.

"What are you reading now, Miss Brinley?" he would ask when they passed in the halls.

"Thackeray," she would reply with an arch smile, having learned he considered the man to be Dickens's intellectual inferior and a much lesser writer.

"Good God!" he'd respond with feigned dismay. "We must do something to correct that. I'll provide you with Mr. Dickens's latest works with all due haste."

The slaves didn't quite know how to deal with her, either. She was a white woman and a lady, and they respected that. However, she was also in service there, and that put her in some nebulous social strata they had never encountered.

Early on, she found that she didn't feel comfortable with being waited on. She asked the squire if it would be acceptable for her to eat in the kitchen alongside the help.

"Well, it's never been done before," he replied.

"Would it give offense or be seen as wrong in my position?"

"Certainly not. Only, perhaps it would be best to not mention it to anyone outside the plantation."

That had been an easy promise to make, since she didn't interact with anyone outside River Hill Hall. Next, she felt that she needed to ask Annie for her permission rather than barge in and impose herself on the busy woman.

"Well, sure thing, miss. I'd enjoy the company," Annie said right away.

Sarah soon came to love and admire the old woman deeply. She had a huge, loving heart and an intuitive, homespun wisdom that Sarah had never encountered before. Her affection for the woman began the moment they met on her first night there. It deepened as she got to know Annie better, gathering more of her history as they sewed together at night by the kitchen fire.

Usually on these occasions, Annie hummed or sang old spirituals, especially her favorite, "Go Down, Moses." Sarah knew that the song was a veiled protest against slavery and a rallying cry for freedom, as were many other spirituals.

Go down, Moses,
Way down in Egypt land.
Tell old pharaoh,
Let my people go.
Let my people go!
Let my people go!
Tell old pharaoh,
Let my people go!

Sarah learned why the song appealed so much to the old woman. One night Annie recounted the tale of how she had been kidnapped as a girl from her village in Africa by warriors from a rival tribe, who had subsequently sold her to a Portuguese slave trader. A brutal transatlantic crossing followed. She was tethered below decks to dozens of other souls, all wallowing in the slime and stink of their collective vomit, feces, and urine.

Despite the misery and filth, sailors often came down into the hold to select a winsome girl, whom they would douse with a bucket of water, then rape. So it was that by the time Annie found herself on the auction block in Louisville several months later, she was with child. As such, she was considered by buyers to be a special bargain because she would be "two slaves for the price of one."

The old squire had bought her to be a personal maid and companion for his wife, who died in childbirth several years after Annie arrived at the plantation. She had then become nursemaid to that child, the squire, and from there she had worked her way up into the respected position of housekeeper. Now sixty-five, she not only served at River Hill Hall, but in many ways, she *was* the hall, embodying its values of hard work, hospitality, and loyalty to loved ones. Sarah was moved by the fact that despite the hardships she'd endured, the old matriarch seemed to harbor no resentments toward anyone, even her captors.

"That bump in my belly when I was standin' on the auction block was my only child, Zeke, who runs the master's ferry now. I didn't care how I come by him. He couldn't be blamed for it. I knew once I felt him there that I'd love him till the day I died, no matter what. I sure am proud of him and how much the master trusts him. And he gave me two beautiful grandsons, Jesse and Lije. How could I not give thanks for that?"

Sometimes Sarah's mind reeled at the power of Annie's stories, all told so matter-of-factly over tea and stitchery, as if she were recounting how she had baked a loaf of bread that morning. Sarah had met many freed slaves at her father's abolitionist meetings but never anyone as inspiring as Annie, who was still a slave but living with it in grace and dignity. The woman soon became a dear friend and true heroine to her.

She also appreciated the additional background Annie gave her about the squire and his family. The old woman proudly recounted what a bright boy he had been, although mischievous. Sarah sensed from the affection in her voice that Annie loved the man as much as she did her own children.

"That child was so smart and curious about everything, he just couldn't stay out of trouble. He was always exploring, always tinkering with things, trying to figure out how they worked or how to make them work better. The old squire about had a fit when the boy took apart his favorite clock. Lucky thing, the child also got it put back together."

She went on to recount how the squire's curiosity and intelligence later paid off in ways that were more productive. He earned a law degree from Transylvania College in Lexington, returned to Louisville to practice, and eventually became a judge. When his father died, the young squire took up full-time management of the plantation.

"And ever since, there's been no finer place in these parts," Annie boasted. "The squire took this property and made it the busiest, richest plantation in the valley."

Along the way, Annie reported, he also fell in love with the daughter of a wealthy shipping magnate from Charleston. The couple adored each other, and spent every minute they could together. However, their marriage hadn't been blessed with offspring, at least not for a long while.

"Those young folks wanted children so bad, but she kept losing them. The family plot is filled with their little gravestones. They'd plumb given up when—Lord be praised—she finally had the young master, Benjamin Booth Junior . . . our Benjie."

That was where Sarah's greatest challenge began. She had been prepared to work with a child who was in shock over the loss of his mother. However, she wasn't prepared to find him a wild, unreachable creature

Following breakfast on the day after her arrival, Annie had come to Sarah with a troubled face. "I reckon it's time for you to meet our l'il boy. All I ask is that you not make any decisions about him yet, not till you get to know him good."

Sarah was puzzled by the request but followed Annie up to the third floor nursery right across from her own rooms. As they neared the door, she heard the sound of a dog growling inside and threw Annie a questioning look. The woman shook her head sadly and opened the nursery door.

Sarah's first impression of the nursery was that it was another lovely, impeccably appointed room at River Hill Hall. Bright sunlight poured into it from the leaded dormer windows all around. The gabled walls were papered with a buttercup-yellow print, dotted with dancing blue rocking horses. A narrow bed was fashioned to look like a boat and was covered with a plump coverlet where Sarah thought she saw more evidence of Annie's stitchery. The floor was cluttered with toys and puzzles. In the corner, a beautiful, blond-haired, blue-eyed boy sat cross-legged beside a pretty, young Negro woman. She sat crocheting in a rocker, humming a nursery tune.

Sarah stepped into the room, looking for the fearful, growling dog she'd heard, wondering why they would let such a vicious animal around the young master. As she reached the center of the room, she heard the fearful growl again. She turned to see the boy bounding toward her with clawing hands and bared teeth, howling at the top of his lungs. If Annie hadn't interceded, he would have surely reached her and done her serious harm.

Peering out from behind Annie, she watched as the woman deftly turned the boy's back to her, got her large arms around his, and brought him to her breast. There she held him firmly but gently, whispering soothing words to him all the while.

"Now you don't need to go on like this, child. This is your new teacher, and she's gonna be a good friend to you."

Sarah was completely immobilized, not so much frightened, as she was shocked and overwhelmed. She had never experienced anything like this. Suddenly, little details of her correspondence and hiring by the squire leaped from her memory.

She recalled now that he hadn't asked her for any references. While she had thought that odd at the time, she had also been relieved. She didn't have any to give other than a note from her landlady, speaking to her general good character and ladylike ways.

He had also included her steamboat fare in his first letter to her, as if he couldn't wait to get her there. She didn't know what the norms were for wealthy people hiring governesses, but in hindsight, it occurred to her that perhaps the squire had been desperate; the boy he wanted her to teach was a veritable animal without speech, manners, or social skills of any kind.

Her heart sank, and her mind reeled with self-recriminations as she pondered these recollections from behind Annie's skirts. How could she have been so stupid, so easily lulled by the squire's charming ways? All of her initial good feelings about this place and the people in it evaporated, replaced by a despairing sense of betrayal.

Annie seemed to sense some of this and called to the young attendant. "Necie, come here and get this boy, right quick now. Me and the young miss got some things to talk out."

The young woman put aside her needlework and came to take charge of Benjie using the same deft hold that Annie had. Annie took Sarah's elbow and guided her out into the corridor, and onto a sturdy settee. They composed themselves and caught their breath.

"I'm . . . I'm speechless," Sarah managed to get out at last.

"I know, I know," Annie murmured, reaching out to cover Sarah's folded hands with her own calloused ones. "They all are, once they come and see what the boy is like. We hoped maybe you'd be different."

Sarah felt a flash of anger. "Then the squire was lying when he told me you'd never had a governess before?"

Annie bristled. "There's no man more honest in these parts

than the squire! And yes, we had governesses before, but not a one stayed the night after they met the young master. So, squire told you the truth."

She paused and gave Sarah a beseeching look. "What about you, miss? Will you take off before night comes, too?"

Sarah's heart raced. What could she possibly hope to accomplish with the feral creature in the next room, when she had no experience of children or teaching? What had she been thinking, throwing all reason to the wind and transplanting herself to this alien place where the lifestyle and values were so foreign to her own? She needed a lot more information.

"Annie, how long has he been this way? What happened to make him like this?"

The old woman's eyes filled with tears. "Oh, miss, only a few months ago, he was the smartest, sweetest boy you'd ever hope to meet. He walked and talked before he was one, and he taught himself how to read when he was two. Then . . . then, the accident happened." She trailed off, with a face so grief stricken that Sarah felt compelled to switch their folded hands so that now hers covered Annie's.

"We were on our way home after dinner at old Mr. Isaacs's place. The missus, Benjie, and me were in the carriage, the big one the squire only uses for special occasions. Squire was riding alongside on his big stallion like always. Benjie was asleep in my lap, while the missus and squire talked about their plans for the fall garden. It was July Fourth, right before dark, and some boys on the roadside lit off firecrackers. The horses shied and bolted. Jesse was at the reins and couldn't stop them, though he tried with all his might. He's never forgiven himself for that."

She pulled a kerchief from her apron pocket to wipe her eyes and blow her nose. "Squire tried his best to run up beside them and pull them in, and he almost made it. Then we come to a bend in the road—beside a steep hill."

Annie broke down and sobbed with all her might. Sarah pulled her down to sit next to her and put an arm around her shoulders. Finally, the old woman regained control.

"The carriage went over the drop-off and rolled over two, maybe even three times. It's all kind of a blur now. Benjie and me landed in some brush, so we come out all right somehow, only bruised up a little. Jesse, too. He jumped off right before the spill. At first, we couldn't see where the missus was at all . . . then we saw her legs under the rig, covered in blood. Somehow Squire and Jesse got that big carriage off of her. Don't ask me how. Only it was too late. She was gone."

Sarah tightened her grip on Annie's shoulders. "How horrible."

"That's not the worst of it. With all that happened to that carriage, the missus . . . well, her body was tore up awful bad. She was such a slip of a thing—dainty as a flower. When the men lifted the rig off her, Benjie was the first to see how bad it was, and . . . well, he's never been the same since. It's like he's put a wall around himself to shut out the world. Funny thing is, he didn't cry or scream or anything. He just disappeared somewhere deep inside himself and he's never come out again."

Sarah's stomach lurched. "Oh, my God, how dreadful for him—and all of you."

"Yes'm," Annie nodded. "Squire tries to be strong for the rest of us, but I know that man inside out, and he's still in a world of hurt. I hear him in the night sometimes, sobbing into his pillow, trying to hide his grief. I wish men didn't fear their own tears. It's not fair and it's not natural. Tears are meant to be shed."

They both sat in silence for a while. Sarah thought about the urbane, humorous man she considered the squire to be stifling his sadness for the sake of his family, and her heart broke for him.

Eventually Annie dried her eyes again and ventured a tentative glance at Sarah. "So, miss, when do you think you might be leavin' today?"

Sarah gazed back at her and saw the wise old eyes weighing the situation and her. She had never wanted anything more in her life than to flee these premises, and she knew Annie was testing her. However, for her to go now after learning the full tragedy that had transpired would be unconscionable. She would never be able to live with herself. She gazed back at Annie and tried to project a confidence she didn't feel.

"Me, leave here? I don't know what you're talking about. I've started a new job, and I'm going to make a success of it."

Annie teared up again. "Oh, thank you, miss, and God bless you. You won't be sorry, I promise you. That li'l boy still got his old self somewhere inside. We just gotta find some way to coax it back out."

"Yes, I'm sure of it," Sarah said with false bravado, all the while thinking, *but how?*

CHAPTER 6

The rest of that day, Sarah spent most of her time in the library, scanning the shelves for something, *anything* having to do with child rearing. To her dismay, she found the rich vault sadly lacking in that particular department. A few books offered a decidedly Victorian bent on how to raise well-behaved and mannerly children to be productive members of society. She found these moralistic primers woefully inadequate to the task.

"What I need is a book on how to turn a demon back into a human being," she murmured to herself.

Annie was tending the fire nearby, but dropped what she was doing and turned to her with a scowl. "For one thing, that child's no demon. He's heartbroken and sick is all. For another, we already tried that. Squire had a priest and a Baptist minister, and old Mr. Isaacs even sent a rabbi out to pray over him. None of them did any good."

If Sarah had harbored any doubts that Annie truly did reign supreme here, they were resolved by the reprimand she'd just received. She felt ashamed of herself.

"Please forgive me, Annie. I was speaking half in jest actually, but you're right, it wasn't fair—or kind."

Annie sniffed and turned back to stoking the fire, but Sarah sensed she'd been mollified. Moreover, she was touched by the woman's loyalty to the boy.

"Annie, what happened when they said the prayers over Benjie?"

Annie turned to her with another scowl. "He only got more worked up, that's what. He screamed and howled like some wild animal, and when they were done, he was worse for days. It took weeks to get him back to what you see now."

"And how did you do that?"

Annie smiled a little at last. "Well, he and Lije have always been real close. I thought if nobody else could do it, maybe Lije could get through to him. And it worked!"

"How?"

Annie beamed with pride. "When they were real small, they had their own language, made up their own words that only they understood, and they chattered away all day like that. When I remembered that, I had Lije play with him every day and talk like they used to together. Before long, Benjie come back around . . . but he was still no better than he was after the accident."

Sarah knit her brows, and an idea came to her. "Do they still play like that?

"No, miss. Lije started his work with me right after that, and he hasn't had time to."

Sarah went out on a limb and risked another tongue-lashing. "Surely helping the young master is more important than training for some future job, especially at such a young age."

Rather than take offense, Annie slowly began to smile. "I'm ashamed to say, I never saw it like that. What do you have in mind?"

"I'm not sure . . . yet," Sarah had to admit. "I'm thinking that if Lije could get through to him *once* that way, maybe he could get through to him again the same way. Let's put our minds to it for a day or two and see what we can come up with."

Annie broke into a huge grin. "I'm real glad you stayed on, miss. You're just what the doctor ordered."

Sarah smiled back at her, glad to be out of the proverbial doghouse. She only wished she felt more sure herself about their chances of reaching the boy.

Within a few days, Sarah had an idea. Eager to seek Annie's judgment on the plan, she hurried to find her. When she did, the housekeeper was shaking out another new quilt and hanging it over the rail of the verandah. Sarah thought back through her memory and realized that this must be the second quilt she had seen Annie hang out in a short time. She paused to admire it.

"My goodness, Annie, another quilt? You're a one-woman quilt-making *factory*."

"Thank you, miss. I do enjoy my stitchery."

Sarah noticed something special about this particular quilt. She ventured a hand forth, and let her fingers wander across the fabric.

"You do such lovely work on them, too, Annie. Why, with this one here, for instance, it's almost as if it's telling a story about a journey of some kind."

Annie shot her a nervous sidelong glance. "Oh, no, miss. You give me too much credit. These are only things you see all the time around here."

Sarah was puzzled by her reaction; she had never known Annie to seem nervous about anything. However, she shrugged her shoulders. "Well, if you say so. Still, it's not like any other quilt I've ever seen. And somehow, whether you meant it to tell a story or not, I bet you that other people are going to see a story of some kind there, too. This block here looks like a rowboat and this one over here like a wagon wheel. Then there's this one with squiggly lines coming out from the center that looks like winding trails in a forest somewhere. There's so much going on in it, it begs one to follow along to see where it all ends up."

Annie became truly agitated. "Now miss, I thank you kindly, but please don't ever say that to anyone else. *Promise me, please?*"

Sarah was completely perplexed but nodded her assent. "Well, all right then, if you insist, I won't say a word."

All she could imagine was that Annie was being overly modest about her work, but the strange interaction stuck with her and tickled her curiosity. Remembering her original mission in coming to find Annie, she changed the topic.

"Annie, I have the germ of an idea and a whole lot of questions. What did Benjie enjoy more than anything in the world before the accident?"

Annie didn't need a moment to consider. "Horses. He was down in the stables all the time with Jesse and Lije. He'd helped groom them and pet them and feed them carrots. Squire had him up in the saddle in front of him from the time he was tiny, then got him his own pony when he turned five."

Her face softened with happy memories for a moment, then clouded.

"After the accident, he wouldn't go near the stables, and the only way he'll have anything to do with horses now is when he's with his daddy. Somehow, if his daddy is there, he'll ride behind him, though he won't go anywhere near a carriage or buggy. They'd go to town sometimes to see Mr. Isaacs . . . well, at least till the old man died. Last time they went in was to welcome young Mr. Isaacs to town, the same night you got here."

"Yes, I remember," Sarah said. Recalling the stares that she and "the young Mr. Isaacs" had attracted on the boat, she decided to keep the fact that she knew him to herself. She forged on with her questions.

"What do you think would happen if, to start with, I only approach Benjie with Lije at my side? And what if Lije teaches me some of their secret words so that I can talk to him in their special language, too? And what if the three of us all go down together to the stables and do what Benjie liked to do more than anything in the world before the accident, groom the horses, and all of that?"

She suddenly realized she had been talking very rapidly and now found herself breathless. For a minute, Annie looked at her in surprise, then began to chuckle.

"Well, it may not help, but it sure can't hurt. Let's try it and see."

The next morning, Sarah sat down with Lije at the big trestle table in the kitchen after breakfast.

"Lije, please, do you think you can teach me to talk with Benjie the way you do? You know, in the special language that you have?"

Lije broke out one of his radiant grins. "Stumble nook, Bama," he said.

Sarah stared at him, befuddled.

"Of course, miss," he translated.

On an impulse, she hugged him. "Oh, Lije, I think I love you."

Impatient, Annie, Lije, and Sarah all trooped up the stairs to the nursery later that morning, exactly in that order, per Annie's insistence.

"I can handle him best if he's in one of his moods," she explained.

Sarah was all too glad to comply, although she was embarrassed to be hiding behind the housekeeper and an eight-year-old boy.

As before, Annie opened the nursery door slowly and peered into the room first. Once more, Necie, the young nursemaid, was there rocking and crocheting. Rather than sitting at her feet, Benjie was in the middle of the room with his arms outstretched, spinning in circles. As he did, he made a singsong noise like a bird chirping. When he noticed the three visitors standing on the threshold, he stopped and dropped his hands to his sides.

At first, he eyed them suspiciously but without any apparent anger or aggression. Slowly, he smiled at Lije.

"Meh adda," Lije said to Benjie, then whispered "my friend," under his breath to Sarah.

Benjie came a couple of steps toward them but still hung back, on his guard. "Meh adda," he replied to Lije, and Sarah had to contain herself from clapping her hands with excitement.

"Meh adda," Lije said again, pointing to Sarah.

Benjie frowned and shook his head. "Nan tana, *nopada!*"

"Not so, *stranger*," Lije translated again, and Sarah was crestfallen. Then she reminded herself they had only now started a complex, challenging process. At least the boy wasn't hurling himself at her again with bared teeth. She decided to take a chance and stepped from behind Lije to stand at his side.

"Nopada," she said, putting her hand to her heart and nodding. She hoped to acknowledge to Benjie that, yes, she was a stranger for now. Taking another chance, she took two small steps to the side, then stopped and said, "Meh adda." She hoped to convey that one might be a stranger one moment but become a friend the next.

She was astonished to see that he understood, for he put his hands over his ears and shook his head.

"Namas, namas!" he shouted.

She turned to Lije who whispered the words, "Never, never."

She realized that she needed to show respect for Benjie's feelings rather than force herself on him. She put her hands over her heart and nodded sadly, looking down at the floor in a submissive way.

Annie jumped in. "Don't be downhearted, miss. You're *talking* with him, and that hasn't happened with anyone but Lije in almost a year—not even his daddy. Do you think maybe that's enough for one day?"

"Precisely my thoughts," Sarah said, and bowed her head slightly to Benjie as she backed out of the room, followed closely by Annie and Lije.

Out in the hall again, they all burst into excited chatter.

"I never saw anything like it!" Annie exclaimed.

Lije nodded agreement. "He looked you in the eye, miss. He *never* does that."

Sarah was almost beside herself with pleasure. "You made it possible, Lije, and I'm so very grateful to you."

"What are we gonna do next, miss?" Annie asked.

Sarah had to confess she hadn't thought of that yet. "I don't know. We don't want to rush him, but I don't want to lose steam, either. You know him best, Lije. What do you think?"

Lije puffed up with pride at being deferred to by an adult. "Do you ride, miss?"

Sarah frowned. "Why, yes, but not since I was a child, and not very well then, I'm afraid. Why do you ask?"

"I think young master needs to see you on horseback next time you meet," he said with assurance.

Annie and Sarah locked delighted eyes and then both hugged the boy simultaneously.

CHAPTER 7

That evening, near supper time, Sarah heard a firm knock on her door and opened it to find the squire there. She thought that he looked a bit discomfited to be so close to her boudoir.

"Forgive the intrusion, Miss Brinley, but would you be so kind as to join me and a friend for dinner? I wanted to ask you personally rather than send someone else to do it, so that you would understand it would be a special favor to me . . . and my friend."

She was half bemused and half amused, to see the master behaving so awkwardly. "Why, of course—thank you. Although I have no eveningwear. Is this formal?"

"No, certainly not. What you have on now will do fine. In the dining room then, say, eight o'clock this evening?" He made a little bow and beat a hasty retreat.

Closing the door behind her, she puzzled for a moment over what had just happened. *What was up?* All she could do was wait and see.

As the appointed hour drew near, she did her best to spruce herself up, putting a tortoiseshell comb in her hair and her mother's favorite brooch on her collar. More than a little nervous, she headed down the long walnut stairway to the formal dining room on the first floor. When she arrived, she was surprised and pleased to see who the squire's friend was.

"Mr. Isaacs, how nice," she exclaimed. It was the first time she had seen someone she already knew and liked, in this land of new relationships.

He came to her and took her hand, smiling warmly. "How very good to see you again, Miss Brinley."

The squire stepped out from behind Samuel and grinned at Sarah. "Surprised?"

Indeed she was, not only by Samuel's unexpected presence, but by the decidedly playful manner of the master as well.

"To be sure," she said. "I suppose Mr. Isaacs explained to you that we met on the boat in transit, as we were about to disembark in Louisville."

"I did," Samuel said.

"He did," the squire said at exactly the same moment, and they all laughed.

"Will you have a seat please, Miss Brinley?" the squire said, pulling out a chair from the gleaming mahogany table.

She went to him and sat at the proffered chair, then let him move her closer to the table. As he leaned over her to do so, she became aware of his nice, clean, masculine scent—mainly leather and horses and a spicy shaving soap. Something about the nearness of him made her even more nervous, and she coughed into her hand.

"What a nice service you have," she said, hoping to cover the unquiet energy she was feeling.

The table was indeed set with the hall's best silver and china. Several large, cut glass candelabras filled the room with a golden glow. However, a small crease appeared between the squire's eyebrows at her compliment.

"Yes, some of my wife's family heirlooms," he said with a tight smile. "Wine, Miss Brinley? Wine, Samuel?"

Sarah was embarrassed to admit she'd never tasted wine, so she accepted a glass. Her finishing school training had been that true ladies rarely partook of alcohol, so she took tiny sips, nursing a single glass of wine through most of the evening.

Annie and Lije were their servers, and once the diners' glasses had been filled, they settled into conversation. The three of them all gathered around one end of the table. The close seating arrangements soon fostered an amiable, informal feeling.

Sarah found that Samuel and the squire were lively conversationalists, each with a dry, rather jaundiced sense of humor that they enjoyed inflicting on one another. At the same time, it also became apparent to her that they liked and respected each other greatly, despite their widely divergent views on many things—from politics, to the economy . . . to slavery.

As the meal progressed, she also found that it felt strange to have Annie and Lije wait on her. She had spent so many enjoyable meals and teas with them, more like a peer than a guest, at the big kitchen table. Lije was coming along well in his training to become a butler or valet, and he performed his serving duties with great skill and dignity. Annie didn't need to give him a single reminder as she oversaw every detail and served the diners alongside him. Sarah realized that if she needed to call on Lije to help her with Benjie for a while, it probably would make little difference in his development as a house server, as he was already quite proficient.

The meal started with a salad of spring greens, and continued with a fish course of fried catfish from the nearby Ohio; a meat course of thick slabs of tender country ham and roasted venison, all served with piping hot side dishes of mashed yams and roasted winter squash. They finished with a huge slice of Annie's jam cake with whipped cream, along with coffee, brandy, and aperitifs. Sarah was stuffed by the time the dessert dishes were cleared away.

As the evening progressed, the conversation moved from local social and government events to predictions about the coming year's crops. Eventually, it moved to worries about the rising tensions between the North and South.

As both an employee and a Northerner, whose opinions would almost certainly be considered unwelcome, Sarah tried to keep her tongue. However, it grew harder as the evening wore on, especially when the topic changed to states' rights.

Samuel and the squire debated the constitutional aspects of the matter, the former citing articles in the document to defend the supremacy of the federal government, and the latter doing the same to argue for the primacy of the states. She found she could no longer restrain herself and butted in.

"Debates about various articles in the Constitution always miss an important point. The founders foresaw the need for the Constitution to be a changing thing when they made provisions for it to be amended in the face of new developments and needs. So, whatever it says about states' rights now could and should change at any time."

The two men set down their brandy snifters and eyed her with a combination of surprise, amusement, and respect. It occurred to her that they had probably never heard a woman airing such a strong political opinion in the presence of men. Finally, Samuel broke the tension. "Well, Benjamin, it seems we've both been taught a lesson by your son's new governess."

They all laughed. Glancing over at Annie, who was watching the interaction from her station by the sideboard, Sarah thought she saw a gleam of approval in her eyes.

The squire stood and raised his glass for a toast. "Speaking of my son's new governess, I'm told she worked a major miracle with him today. My deepest gratitude to you, Miss Brinley."

Samuel rose, too, and the men leaned in to touch their brandy snifters to the aperitif glass in Sarah's hand. "Here, here!" Samuel cheered.

Sarah felt the blood rise to her cheeks and was deeply uncomfortable. "It's nothing to do with me. Lije made it all happen. We may get nowhere tomorrow."

"And what is planned for tomorrow?" the squire asked anxiously.

Since she was figuring things out as she went, she felt more and more uncomfortable with the direction the conversation was taking.

"Lije seems to think Benjie might warm to me better if he sees that I'm a capable horsewoman. He wants me to come down to the stables in the morning and work with Jesse on my riding skills."

The squire glanced over at Annie—Lije had already been dismissed to go to bed—and gave her an approving nod.

"Smart fellow, that Lije," he said, and Sarah saw Annie beam with pride.

Samuel surprised them. "May I invite myself to come along? I've spent years up North at rabbinical school, seldom going out anywhere, and never had any reason to learn how to ride. Now

I find that I have to pay a hackney driver to take me anywhere I want to go, and it would be so much nicer if I could jump on horseback and take myself there."

The squire broke into a sly smile and slowly swirled his brandy in his glass. "Oh, please, by all means, *do*, my friend. I *can't wait* to see this."

"So be it," Samuel replied, coolly swirling his brandy glass in return. "Be there tomorrow morning, so you can observe me riding like a cavalry soldier."

Sarah watched the two friends sparring with each other. *Oh, my, what's going to come of this?*

The big clock in the library began to strike, and as Sarah counted the chimes, she realized that it was eleven o'clock. Looking over at Annie again, she saw her covering a yawn behind her hand. A quick stab of guilt went through her as she realized that they were keeping this tired woman up late while they enjoyed themselves in idle conversation.

She was reminded once more that this plantation she had already begun to love was still a slave operation. The workers on it, no matter how well they might appear to be treated, were still powerless victims of an inhumane way of life that made them subject to the whims of rich, white people. A wave of anger swept over her, and she felt her eyes starting to well up.

"What is it, Sarah?" Samuel asked.

"Yes," the squire said. "Your face just went completely white."

She knew that the diplomatic, smart thing to do was demure. "It's nothing. I thought of something sad."

However, as soon as the words escaped her lips, she felt dishonest. She raised her chin and squared her shoulders.

"Actually, there is something more than that. We're keeping

a tired, hard-working woman up, while we sit here and enjoy ourselves, and it made me very sad."

Samuel shot her an appreciative look, but kept his silence, and continued swirling his brandy snifter. The squire, however, was another matter. His brow furrowed and his face clouded.

"My, my, Miss Brinley, it appears I'm being taught yet another lesson, this time on how to manage my household and my people."

More challenging words leapt from her lips before she knew it. "If they truly were people to you, they'd be free, wouldn't they?"

The darkness in his eyes grew deeper. "Careful, Miss Brinley," he said through clenched teeth, and she realized she had crossed a dangerous line. She also realized that, whatever her real feelings on this or any other matter having to do with managing the plantation, she was an employee and had no right to interfere. She knew she needed to try to make amends.

"I . . . I don't mean to judge and I can't thank you enough for including me in this wonderful evening. I can't think of a time when I've enjoyed myself more. In truth, I don't think there's ever been one."

She stopped, uncertain where to go next. Then she sighed, and her shoulders sagged. She knew she had to do something to try to recapture the good spirits they had been enjoying earlier. It was time for her to be more honest.

"I already told you my father was an academic, but I didn't mention that he was also an abolitionist. I grew up attending meetings where speakers railed against the evils of slavery. I met escaped slaves at some of these meetings, and the stories they told broke my heart—and sickened and *angered* me, as well."

She ventured a glance at the squire and was relieved to see that, although he was still scowling, he also seemed to be listening closely to what she was saying. She felt a bit reassured.

"I met men—and women too—who had so many scars from whippings on their backs that the skin looked like a newly-plowed field. I met others who were missing hands because they'd stolen food or tongues because they'd talked back to their masters."

A wave of revulsion swept over her as she remembered these encounters, and she suddenly wished she'd never opened her mouth.

"So, when my parents left me penniless, I had to do something to make a living, and that led me to answer your advertisement. Now I don't know what I was thinking at the time. I mean, I *like* children, but I'd never had much to do with them. It simply seemed like something I could figure out how to do."

She stole another glance at the squire and was encouraged to see he was no longer scowling. She reached a hand out to him across the polished table surface.

"You were the first—and, honestly, the *only* person—to answer my correspondence. And so, here I am. The only thing is, I hadn't fully considered the slavery issue. I didn't even remember Kentucky was a slave state until I recalled that *Uncle Tom's Cabin* was set here."

She looked across the table at Samuel and saw him watching her with a look she thought signaled friendship and respect. She decided she should finish and take her leave—from this table and, if need be, this house.

"Samuel predicted this tension when we first met on the *Eclipse*, though I never expected it to bubble up like it did tonight. Please forgive me, if I was . . . disrespectful. That wasn't my intent, truly. I am learning so many new ways here, and sometimes I feel that I'm not learning them very well."

She stopped, folded her hands, and looked down at them. The long silence that ensued was even more frightening to her than the squire's anger had been. Finally, he broke the quiet.

"I applaud your morals, Miss Brinley, and regret that my own are not so highly developed. Perhaps it would be . . . *helpful* for you to have a bit more information."

He looked toward the sideboard and noticed that Annie was now fully alert and listening to this provocative discussion. Smiling dryly, he said, "Join in any time you want to, Annie. I could use a little help here." Then he resumed addressing Sarah.

"The first thing I need you to know, Miss Brinley, is that I have never bought or sold a single slave and that I have sworn before God, and man, that I never will. I abhor the institution of slavery. Everyone here at River Hill is a worker my father purchased and bequeathed to me as part of my inheritance, or one who was born here to those workers, like Jesse, and Lije. When I die, they will all be freed."

"Then why not free them now, if you feel so strongly about these matters?"

She had blurted something out again and wished that she could control her tongue better.

She heard the rustling of Annie's starched petticoats coming up behind her and turned to see the woman's wise brown eyes looking down on her kindly.

"Who says I want to be free, miss? My kin are all here with me, and we all have work we enjoy, mostly anyways. And it means the world to us that squire is never gonna sell any of us away from each other. Yes'm, I'm tired tonight, but I also enjoy times like this. They remind me of when the missus was alive."

"If you were free you could have your own place, Annie, and live your life the way you want to," Sarah countered.

"But *this is* my own place and the way I want to live, miss. I've been through a lot, and I've seen a lot of sad, troubled times. I scarce ever think about any of that these days because I feel so safe here. Oh, sure, it's been a hard, heavy load since the missus left us. But the hall is a happy, pretty place to be—for the most part. Why question fate? Why not take one day at a time and let all the rest sort itself out?"

Sarah looked across the table for support from Samuel, but he seemed to be as surprised as she was by the complex rhetoric flying about the room.

The squire jumped back in. "Besides, how would I run this place without my people? I could never afford to pay them. There are times when I can barely afford to feed them. Slavery is an economic necessity in the South, and that trumps any moral issues surrounding it for planters."

"Why, you're *rich*," Sarah said.

The squire laughed out loud. "Let me take you to my banker so you can tell him that, and give him a good laugh, too. Yes, I have land and property and slaves, but working this fertile bottomland, right beside an unpredictable river, is always a gamble. There are years when it's underwater much of the spring, and we can't plant any crops on some of it. What we can grow in the kitchen garden, and the game we can hunt, or the livestock we can slaughter only go so far. Mouths still have to be fed and taxes still have to be paid, even during the lean years."

Sarah had never considered these aspects of plantation life. "I never thought of it that way. It all seems so . . . so *bountiful*, and comfortable here. I never considered that a slave might not want to be free. Before now, the only ones I ever met risked their lives for their freedom." She was relieved to see the squire's face soften.

"You're young and you have the hopeful ideals of the young. That's a good thing, especially after all the losses you've been through this last year."

She almost teared up with relief, but frowned as his face darkened again and he continued with a sad smile.

"If we're lucky, our ideals stay fresh and optimistic, guiding us throughout our lives. However, sometimes our ideals have to be tempered, or even sacrificed entirely, against life's harsh realities."

"Like the loss of your wife and Benjie's illness," she ventured.

"That's true, to be sure, but even far more than that. We live in dangerous times, miss. This nation is a powder keg about to explode at any minute. There's even talk of it coming completely apart. If that happens, there will be losses and suffering such as the world has never seen, losses that will make yours and mine pale in comparison."

She felt a shiver as he talked and put her arms around herself. He noticed and seemed to come to himself.

"What kind of host am I? Talking on and on about morbid matters like war and suffering. And you're right about one thing at least. Annie does look tired, so I say let us all retire and let her get her rest."

They rose and moved to the stairs in the hallway. As she turned to go up, Sarah felt a light touch on her shoulder.

"Speaking of wars, do we have a truce?" the squire asked.

She had to laugh at the mischievous gleam in his eyes. In spite of his age and usual gravitas, it seemed to her that he sometimes exuded the energy of a naughty boy. "Of course we do. Am I forgiven for being so rude and opinionated?"

"Nothing to forgive. You spoke the truth as you saw it . . . a bit more, uh, strongly than we're used to from ladies in these parts. Yet you conceded that you have things to learn, and, clearly, you are learning them. You have earned my utmost respect for that and for what you've accomplished with my son today. However, now I must take my leave from both of you. One of my best broodmares is foaling and I want to check on her before retiring. Good night." He turned and abruptly left.

Sarah looked at Samuel, puzzled. "Well, that was sudden."

Samuel didn't seem puzzled in the least but hesitated before responding, picking his words carefully when he did. "I think perhaps there may be more to the squire than any of us can imagine."

They remained there for a while chatting about the fine meal they had just had and their riding lesson the next day. Soon, Sarah noticed Samuel fidgeting.

"What is it, Samuel?"

He seemed relieved she asked. "I think I'm going to go after Benjamin to see if I can help in any way. Goodnight, miss."

He left as abruptly as the squire had. As she turned again to go up the stairs, Sarah saw Annie come in the back hall door from the verandah carrying a folded quilt in her arms. It was the same one she had admired earlier, the one Annie had been so unaccountably nervous about. However, holding it to her breast now, the woman had a calm, contented look. She was once more singing her favorite spiritual, "Go Down, Moses," and looked thoroughly happy. Sarah was thoroughly confused.

What is going on here tonight? It's like we're all under some sort of spell.

She shook her head to clear it, waved goodnight to Annie, and hurried up to her bed.

CHAPTER 8

Despite the truce she had struck with the squire, Sarah had trouble getting to sleep that night. She tossed and turned, blaming it on drinking too much coffee with dinner. Benjie also appeared to be having a rough night, for she heard him cry out in his sleep several times. She was finally beginning to drift off when a loud noise startled her awake. She sat up in bed, trying to figure out what it had been. Was it thunder? She didn't recall seeing storm clouds that evening.

She rose from her bed, wrapped a shawl around her shoulders, and went to the window. At first, she couldn't see anything, for it was a moonless night; then she thought she saw a glimmer of light coming from the riverbank not far away. Soon she was sure of it, for the light came closer. Before long, she saw a group of men following another man carrying a lantern—and they all had rifles slung over their shoulders. With a sudden prickle of alarm, she realized they were coming to the hall.

She went to get her clothes from the wardrobe and threw them on as quickly as she could. As she did, she heard a loud banging coming from the back hallway. Someone was pounding the verandah door hard enough to break it down, and the angry intensity of the sound alarmed her further.

Benjie seemed to be even more alarmed than she for she heard him screaming in fright. She rushed out to the hallway and found Necie trying to comfort him in the doorway of the nursery.

"What is it, miss?" the young woman asked, looking as frightened as the child she was holding.

"I don't know, Necie, but I'm going down to find out."

"Be careful, miss. Something's not right down there."

Sarah shuddered at the idea, but tightened her shawl around her shoulders and hurried in the darkness down the two flights of stairs. When she reached the first floor, she saw candlelight coming from the back hall and turned to find the squire, Annie, and Jesse all huddled together in a hushed, urgent conversation. The pounding on the door beside them continued, and she heard someone shouting through it.

"Sheriff's office! Open this door!"

The squire noticed Sarah and hurried toward her.

"Miss Brinley, go back upstairs at once."

"Why? What's happening?"

"Nothing I can't handle, so please do as I say."

"But I might be able to help somehow."

He took her by the elbow and, gently but firmly, took her to the foot of the stairs.

"Please, I don't have time to argue," he said tersely, but she thought she saw an unexpected pleading look in his eyes.

"Well, all right, only please call up to me if you need me."

He nodded and left her to return to Annie and Jesse. She went up the stairs with reluctant steps and reached the second floor landing, but as she turned to go up to the third floor, something stopped her in her tracks. Master's orders or not, she didn't feel good about leaving the others downstairs to deal with whatever was happening. Something was gravely amiss, and she wanted to stand by to help in any fashion she could.

She went down the stairway a couple of steps and looked over the banister until she caught sight of the group below. Under the cover of darkness, she felt sure that they couldn't see her. Though they were whispering, she was able to catch pieces of their conversation.

"That's our story," the squire said. "And no matter what they say or do, we're sticking to it. Can we all commit to that?"

"Of course," Annie said.

"You can count on us, sir," Jesse added.

The squire straightened his spine and went to unlatch the door. As soon as it was open, a throng of sweaty, angry men poured into the hall.

The leader of the pack was red-faced with fury. "What is the meaning of keeping us waiting out there so long, sir?"

The squire looked coolly at him. "I believe I'm the one who should be asking the questions here, sir. You've invaded and disrespected my home, my family, and me tonight with no explanation."

The man blustered. "I'm county sheriff, by God. I've got the law behind me. I don't owe you an explanation."

The squire shot back, "Then if you're following the law, sir, you must have a warrant. Let me see it, *now*."

The sheriff lost a bit of his bluster. "No . . . no, I don't, but I don't need one for this. I'm not here to search your house. I'm here looking for a pack of runaways. These men are bounty hunters, and they've had their sights on a group hidin' down on your riverbank. They saw them there earlier tonight, hunkered down in the birch grove, but when they went in to seize them, they was all gone . . . like they vanished into thin air."

The squire stared at him with contempt. "What has that to do with me, and more importantly, my *family?*"

The sheriff lost a bit more of his bluster. "Well, well, it's your land, after all. Those is your woods, and it's against the law to harbor fugitive slaves."

"How dare you suggest such a thing?" the squire said with venom in his voice. "I'm a former judge and leading citizen in Louisville. Are you stupid enough to believe that I would risk all that by harboring runaway slaves? Why, I could have your job for even insinuating it."

The sheriff was totally out of his league. He hadn't expected any opposition to his authority.

"Now, now, not so fast, sir. I'm just upholding the law. These men came to me earlier, and asked me to accompany them on this raid tonight, as is proper in my position, keepin' it all legal, ya' know. When we got here, the runaways was gone, but we did see someone moving about in the woods. We called on him to stop and come forward but he ran. We shot at him and thought we heard someone shout, but when we got to where he should've been, no one was there. Nothing but this."

He held out a bloodied pearl gray silk cravat, and Sarah gasped at the sight of it. The last time she had seen it, Samuel was wearing it. Fortunately, no one below heard her.

The squire pressed the advantage he had gained on matters of manners and legal authority. "I own hundreds of acres here, you ignorant man. Can you honestly believe that I know or am personally responsible for everything that happens on my land? I ride it every day, seeing to various needs, and along the way, I notice all kinds of things I didn't ordain. Poachers take my game, vagrants fish from my dock without my permission. Where are you, 'the law,' when *these* things happen on my land?"

At that, the sheriff totally deflated. "I'm . . . I'm a busy man, sir. I can't see to everything that goes on in my district."

The squire bristled. "Yet you can come onto my land, uninvited, then storm up to pound on my door in the middle of the night, frightening my child and staff from their beds, all at the request of a bunch of *bounty hunters*? Who is your allegiance to, sir? These dregs of humanity, or a taxpaying, *voting* resident of your own county?"

The bounty hunters began grousing. "Are you goin' to let him talk about us like that?"

By this time, the sheriff wanted nothing more than to escape with whatever remaining dignity he could muster.

"Well, of course, my loyalty is to you, sir. I think our job here is done as we've found out all we need to find out, so we'll be goin' now." He tipped his hat and headed for the door against the protests of the other men.

"If you can't search him or his place, can't you at least ask where he's been tonight?"

The sheriff turned in the doorway with a beseeching look. "Well, sir, that would be all right to ask, wouldn't it?"

The squire sneered. "Not that I'm obliged to answer, but I was down at the stables helping one of my thoroughbred mares with a difficult foaling."

Sarah noticed his attire for the first time. He was indeed uncharacteristically disheveled. His elegant linen shirt was stained with sweat, mud covered his breeches, and his riding boots were wet with muck.

"Well, then, that's good enough for me, sir. We'll be off now."

The squire stopped him with a rough hand on his sleeve. "Oh, no, you won't. You owe my family an apology."

The sheriff looked beyond the squire at Annie and Jesse. "All I see here is slaves. They ain't none of your family."

"Oh, yes, they are. Apologize to them." He turned to the bounty hunters. "And you, too." An angry rumble went through the gathering.

"I ain't apologizin' to *them*."

"When pigs fly."

The squire went to the door and slammed it shut. "No one is leaving this house until they apologize to my family for frightening them. If they don't, I believe it will be your legal duty, sheriff, to go and fetch the mayor to arbitrate this matter."

The sheriff turned and shouted at the indignant bounty hunters. "Apologize! You have no idea what kinda' trouble you're stirrin' up here, and I ain't losin' my job over the likes of you!"

The group grumbled, but one by one, each came forward and rendered some sort of poor apology, speaking to the room at large.

"Didn't mean ta' scare no one."

"Got kids m'self. Sorry we woke yor'n."

The squire smiled grimly. "I should insist you look my people in the eyes, but if it means getting rid of you at once, that will have to suffice. Now, *go*."

They grumbled a bit more, but they all complied. When the last man had exited onto the verandah, the squire started to close the door, but the sheriff stopped him.

"You may've run me off tonight, sir, but I'll be back. I got my eye on you, an' this place now, an' there's somethin' funny goin' on here that I don't like. I don't know what it is yet, but I'll find out. Mark my words, I *will* find out."

The squire reached out and pushed him firmly in the chest. "Get off my land *this instant* or I will go and wake the mayor myself."

The sheriff's eyes widened and he shouted to the men behind him. "All right boys, outta here *now!*" They scurried off like roaches as the squire slammed the door closed.

Once it was shut, the three confederates raced down the hall to the library. Sarah tiptoed down the stairs to the doorway and covered her mouth to stifle another gasp at what she saw.

Stretched out on a chaise, Samuel lay unconscious and bleeding, a gaping hole in his left shoulder. Lije was holding a wadded cloth to it, pressing down hard, his eyes wide with fright. Annie moved him aside and began working on Samuel herself. After a few moments, she shook her head.

"I can't stop the blood, sir. We may have to fetch the doctor."

"Keep trying, Annie. I don't think it's an artery because the flow isn't pulsing. And the lead appears to have passed clean through him. If we have to call a doctor, the whole county will know by morning what's happened here tonight, and we can't risk that."

"I'll try, sir. Jesse, run get my medicine bag. I need some alum. And Lije, you head off to bed now, you hear me?"

Jesse ran from the room with Lije trotting behind him. They bumped into Sarah on their way out. "Sorry, miss," Jesse said and hurried down the hallway.

The squire heard the exchange and turned to confront her. "I thought I told you to go back to bed."

She raised her chin. "Yes, you did, but I'm not your slave. I'm your *employee*, at least for the present, I hope. And I still have a mind of my own."

She watched the struggle on his face, seeing that he wanted to assert his authority, but also realized that he might need her help.

"All right, then. Come over here and keep track of his pulse."

She did as he ordered, but was soon frightened to find how faint Samuel's heartbeat was. "We need to do something fast, sir, or he's going bleed to death."

Jesse reappeared with Annie's medicine bag, and she rifled through its contents until she found her jar of alum. She quickly packed a poultice of the white powder into Samuel's wound and pressed a clean bandage from her bag over it. While Annie worked on his shoulder, Sarah leaned over Samuel's face and tried to communicate with him.

"Samuel, it's me, Sarah. Can you hear me?"

He was unresponsive. The squire came up beside her and put a hand on her shoulder.

"He's better off this way. If he were conscious, he'd be in unbearable pain."

"My God, sir, what happened out there tonight? This man is the gentlest soul on the planet. How did he come to be in this state?"

"There will be time for explanations later," he replied, grim-faced. "Right now, we need to focus on saving his life."

Annie looked up at them with panic in her eyes. "It's not workin', sir.'"

The squire looked even more grim. "Then we'll have to cauterize the wound."

He went to the hearth, grabbed a poker, and stuck it into

the glowing coals. After several minutes, he pulled it out and grunted with approval at the blueish red metal tip.

"Hold him down, ladies. Unconscious or not, he's going to fight like hell when I do this."

Sarah and Annie took positions holding Samuel down and looked at each other with anxious faces.

The squire walked to Samuel, removed the soaked bandage and poultice Annie had been pressing into him, and muttered under his breath.

"Forgive me, my friend, for what I'm about to do, but it's the only chance we have of saving your life, and this house, tonight." Then he touched the red-hot poker to Samuel's wound and held it there for what seemed an eternity to Sarah.

As he'd predicted, the unconscious man writhed in pain and fought to rise up. It took all of her strength for Sarah to hold him down. Looking across at Annie, she saw the old woman panting as well. The smell of burnt flesh filled the room, and Sarah gagged. Finally, the squire removed the poker and set it back on the hearth.

Sarah looked down at the wound, blackened and smoking, but she was relieved to see that the flow of blood had stopped.

"Thank God," she said.

"Praise Jesus," Annie chimed in.

"No, thank battlefield medics," the squire said. "I saw them do this when I fought in the Mexican War."

They all looked at each for a long moment, and then Sarah passed out.

CHAPTER 9

When she came to, Sarah was lying in her own bed. A golden beam of sunlight played on her face. She stretched and yawned, trying to remember the dream she had awakened from. It wasn't a particularly happy dream, as some sort of crisis was going on, but she couldn't recall details. Suddenly, she sat bolt upright, realizing it hadn't been a dream at all.

The events of the night before came rushing back to her, and she struggled to come to grips with the fact that they had happened at all. How had the peace and tranquility of this beautiful place come tumbling down so abruptly and frightfully? It certainly did seem like some awful nightmare. However, looking at her clothes draped over the chair beside her bed, she saw traces of dried blood on the shawl she had worn last night, and she knew it had been no dream.

She shuddered, rose from her bed, and got into her clothes, leaving the shawl where it was. Perhaps Annie would have some potion for removing bloodstains.

She went into the hallway and listened at the nursery door for a moment. All was quiet within, and she took that as a good sign.

She descended to the second floor and looked at the door to the squire's bedroom. It was ajar, and she could see a young girl making up his bed, so she took that as a good sign, too. The master was apparently out and about, despite the night's travails. Maybe life at the hall was getting back to normal.

She went down to the library and tapped on the closed doors.

"Come in." She was glad to hear Samuel's voice and he sounded surprisingly normal.

She slid open the doors and went to his side. He was bare-chested, propped up on pillows, with a thick, clean bandage over his wound. She tried not to stare at his nakedness but couldn't help noticing that he had a very attractive chest, lightly dusted with auburn hair and rippled with muscle. For the first time, she realized that Samuel was a very handsome man, and felt a sudden, confusing wave of attraction for him. He seemed to intuit something in her glance, and tried to reach for an afghan to cover himself, but it was too far away.

"Let me," she said, laughing, and she arranged the cover over his bare torso. She sat down beside him and ventured the bold move of taking his hands in hers, hoping he wouldn't think her less of a lady for doing so.

"How are you feeling?"

"Honestly? Awful!"

"I'm not surprised," she said. "For a while there last night, we thought we were going to lose you. If the squire hadn't cauterized your wound, I believe we would have."

"I don't remember anything," he said. "I think I'm glad I don't."

She nodded. "So you have no idea what happened?"

"Well, that's not entirely true," he conceded. "I was running across the fields after Benjamin when I lost sight of him. Then I heard a group of men marching up behind me, and I turned and saw that they were armed. I ducked into the forest and hid amongst the birch trees, while they went on down to the riverbank. I heard a lot of shouting and cursing. I started to back out of the woods and run back across the fields to the hall, when somebody ordered me to stop. At that, I took off sprinting with all my might . . . and that's the last thing I remember."

Sarah took in all of this and considered it. "That certainly fits with what the sheriff reported last night. It seems he was on his way there with a bunch of bounty hunters to capture a group of runaway slaves hiding by the river. By the time they got there, the group was gone . . . 'vanished into thin air' were his words. He insinuated the squire had something to do with it, and you've never seen anyone as angry as the squire was, hearing that. He put the sheriff in his place and kicked them off the premises. Still, I worry about what kind of trouble that mean-spirited little man might try to stir up."

They both heard the doors open, and Sarah let go of Samuel's hand. Annie came into the room with Lije, who was carrying a tea tray, smiling with complete confidence.

"I thought there might be some mighty hungry folks in here," Annie said. "I got tea and coffee and sweet cakes for y'all."

Noticing that the room was still faintly redolent with the smell of burnt flesh, Sarah lost her appetite. "Nothing to eat for me, thanks, Annie. I'll just have a cup of tea."

"I'm starving," Samuel declared. "Give me one of everything."

Soon, they were laughing and talking over plates of sweets in their laps. Samuel insisted that even Annie and Lije partake, and the little boy looked like he was celebrating Christmas. Sarah decided that maybe the nightmares of last night had been banished. She would soon find out that she had been terribly wrong.

CHAPTER 10

The next morning she woke up happier, knowing that she was to have her first riding lesson with Jesse. In light of the events on the night of the dinner party, they had canceled it the day before. Samuel was still too indisposed to join in yet. She put on her clothes, realizing as she did that she didn't have a riding habit. Her usual clothes would have to do.

Over her breakfast in the kitchen, Annie told her Jesse was getting a horse ready for her.

Sarah felt a mixture of anxiety and anticipation.

"I do hope it's one that's gentle—and *slow*."

Annie turned from stirring a pot over the fire. "Don't you worry, miss. Jesse knows every horse in those barns, and he'll pick out one that's right for you."

Eager to get her lesson started, Sarah pushed away her breakfast plate and rose to leave. As she did, Annie noticed her clothes.

"You need a riding habit, miss."

"I don't have one. As I told Lije the other day, I haven't ridden since I was a child."

Annie eyed her up and down in an appraising way. "I might have one in storage that'll do. Look for me later today, and we'll see what I've been able to come up with."

Sarah was grateful. "Thank you, Annie. I've never had my own riding clothes, never ridden enough to need them."

"My pleasure, miss. Every lady needs her own habit. Otherwise, her pantalets will show and that wouldn't be proper."

Sarah laughed and headed out to the barns with lighter spirits. Once there, she took a few moments to wander up and down the corridors between the rows of clean, sweet-smelling stalls. The wood was varnished to a glossy sheen, and the stalls had Dutch doors that allowed the horses to poke out their heads, and see what was going on around them.

She had always considered barns to be almost like churches. Exploring the squire's stables, she thought they would surely qualify as cathedrals. Moving from stall to stall, she realized that the squire's horses lived better than many human beings. Their water buckets and the hay cribs in the far corner of each stall were full. The wood shavings that covered the stall floors had recently been changed, and the aisles between the stalls appeared to have just been swept. Each stall door had a brass plate on it where the name of its occupant was engraved.

She was thinking how skilled and hardworking the people who managed all of this were, when Jesse appeared.

"Ready for your lesson, miss?"

"Why, yes. I was admiring the barns first. Is this your handiwork, Jesse?"

"Well, partly. There's a team of grooms who all chip in here, but I'm their foreman, so I guess you could say it's my handiwork."

"I think you're being too modest. This place is immaculate and so well-appointed, much like the rooms at the hall."

A shadow crossed his face. "Well, that would be because the missus laid out these stables and saw to every detail of them.

You see, she loved horses almost as much as she loved Benjie and the squire."

A smile lit his face. "In fact, the squire used to complain that she loved her horses *more* than she loved him. Of course, that wasn't so, but it got him a kiss and a hug from her every time, so he used the ploy a lot."

Though Jesse had volunteered all this information, Sarah felt a combination of sadness, envy, and guilt; grieving to hear once more about the lost wife and mother; jealous that she herself didn't have any of the woman's many admirable talents and traits; and guilty to be eavesdropping in a sense on the privacy of the couples' relationship. It felt intrusive to her.

Uncomfortable, she changed the topic. "Annie says you're picking out a horse for me?"

"Yes, miss, I already have the perfect fit in mind for you."

"Wonderful. When can I ride?"

"Oh, we aren't going to be doing any riding today, miss. Maybe not for a while."

She was perplexed. "How am I ever going to learn to ride then?"

"Come with me, and I'll explain." He led the way through the aisles, giving her the first of her lessons as they went on their way.

"Horseback riding begins on the ground. You have to first form a bond with your mount by grooming, feeding, and walking them on a lead. You talk in a soft, calm voice while you work on their feet or brush out their mane and tail."

A wave of anxiety washed over Sarah. "Work on their *feet?* You mean, pick them up and clean them, *myself?* What if they kick me in the process?"

Jesse smiled patiently. "That's why you want to have a good strong bond with them so they won't want to kick you."

Sarah wasn't so sure. "Isn't that trusting a lot to a big, dumb creature?"

Jesse chuckled. "Oh, horses aren't dumb creatures, miss. No, not at all. Yes, they're big, and have a brain that, for all their size and muscle, isn't very big. Still, they sense things we can't, and they know things we don't, like when a storm's coming, or how to tell whether somebody is trustworthy, merely by the way the person walks and talks and smells."

Sarah was baffled but fascinated. "My goodness, you certainly do know your work, Jesse. I want to learn everything I can from you. How long do you think it will take for me to be a decent horsewoman?"

He smiled again. "Well, I've been at this since I was five, and I'm nineteen now, and I still don't know all there is to know about it. You're a smart lady, though, and you'll soon have enough of the basics to get a good start at it."

She felt disappointed with this response but could also understand it. She had been reading and writing poetry and short stories since she was five, and she didn't know everything about those pursuits. She set her jaw.

"Well, if determination counts for anything, I'm going to do my best to move along as fast as I can. Lije thinks I've got to if I'm ever going to get through to Benjie."

Jesse nodded. "I think we can get you to a place where you can do that sooner rather than later. Now come and meet your new best friend."

He said the last words with a little gleam in his eye. They had reached a stall at the very end of the barn where a great brute of a beast hung his head out through the open top door and watched their approach, nickering a welcome. Sarah saw that the brass plate read Jack of Hearts and wondered what the origins of the name were.

Jesse went up to the horse and stroked his nose. "Are you happy to see us, old boy? Have you missed me?"

The horse nibbled at his fingers with his lips, and Sarah cringed. "Couldn't he take some fingers off with those huge teeth?"

Jesse laughed again. "Well, he could if he had a mind to, but not my Jack. No, this old boy here is the sweetest thing I've ever known. The missus bred him from her favorite hunter-jumper mare, Lady Jane, and the squire's calmest, steadiest thoroughbred stallion, Wind Rider. He's safe as can be. At Benjie's birthday parties, we used to put little children on him, and he babysat them like an old granny."

"Well, all right, if you say so," she said. "I'll believe it when I see it."

Jesse grabbed a couple of curry combs and brushes from a cloth sack hanging beside the stall door and opened the door to let them in. "Follow me, miss, and you'll see soon enough. Jack is a big baby. You're going to love him."

Sarah tiptoed into the stall with tentative steps, trying to quell her nervousness. "Is it true what they say about horses knowing when you're scared of them, that they can smell your fear?"

"I believe so, miss."

"Then I need to convince him I'm not scared, even though I am, right?"

"Yes, miss."

"All right, how do I do that?"

Jesse's patience was boundless. "Start by taking some deep breaths around him. Let him see and hear you doing it. Talk to him like he's an old friend you're having tea with. Chat about the weather and how your day's been going and ask him about his."

Now it was Sarah's turn to laugh. "That sounds a little crazy."

"Yes, it does, miss, and it is a little crazy. All I know is, it works."

Taking some deep breaths, Sarah approached Jack and reached out a hand to stroke his neck. When she made contact with his silky coat, she felt an immediate sense of calm. She continued stroking him gently but firmly to signal to him that she was kind and confident.

"Good boy, Jack, big boy, Jack," she cooed in a lilting voice like a nursemaid might use. "Aren't you a handsome one? Such a nice red coat."

"That's right, miss, exactly like that. And it's called chestnut, that red coat, or some folks call it sorrel."

She continued stroking, and babbling to the horse as she walked all around him. When she got to his hindquarters, she felt a stab of fear, and started to give him a wide berth.

"All right, miss, first correction. When you're walking behind a horse, you want to stay as close to their rump as you can."

She knit her brow. "What if he kicks me?"

"For one thing, Jack won't kick you. For another, if you're dealing with a horse that *would*, the farther you are from his legs when he does kick, the more leverage he's going to have for his hooves to make contact with you and do serious harm. If you stay real close and he kicks, it'll probably only be his haunches that reach you, and that'll simply push you off to his side."

She nodded. "That makes sense in a contrary sort of way."

Jesse smiled approval. "Now that's exactly what you want to keep in mind with horses. A lot of what I'm going to tell you isn't going to make sense at first, but when you think it through and try it out, you'll see that it does work."

She forced herself to circle Jack's rump more closely several times, stroking his haunches and murmuring to him all the while. As she did, she felt her fear of being kicked vanish and smiled with relief.

"You know, it's funny," she said. "I'm talking and petting him, and I can see him breathing slower and his head drooping a little, like he wants to take a nap. Yet, I'm the one who's being soothed here. I haven't felt this relaxed in months."

"That's exactly right, miss. Horses can be great healers. After the accident, the only thing that seemed to help the young master was getting up on horseback with his daddy. He wouldn't ride his own pony by himself anymore, but he would ride behind the squire. And when the boy was on board, that big old fiery stallion walked like he was carrying a load of eggs, picking every footstep as careful as could be."

She narrowed her eyes, musing aloud. "Hmmm . . . you lose your mother in a horrible, horse-related accident, and you're scared to get back on your own horse alone, but you will get up on a spirited stallion with your father."

Jesse listened closely as if he was trying to figure out where she was going.

She eventually shook her head. "You're right, Jesse, it doesn't make rational sense, but somehow it works. Maybe that was what Lije was thinking when he suggested this whole idea."

"I believe so, miss. Now, why don't you take one of these

brushes and give him a nice brisk rubdown. I'll show you how. Then I think we'll call it a day."

She was relieved to be wrapping up what felt like a successful first lesson until he added, "Tomorrow we'll work on shampooing manes and tails and cleaning hooves."

Her heart sank, and she predicted she was probably going to have another restless night.

CHAPTER 11

Arriving back at the hall, Sarah found the squire and Samuel engaged in a somber dialogue over coffee and cigars on the verandah. Whatever they were discussing, they stopped when they saw her coming up the porch steps, and rose to greet her.

"How was your lesson?" Samuel asked.

"Wonderful! I had no idea horses were such complex creatures."

"Jesse is the best teacher anyone could ask for," the squire said. "He understands them inside and out."

She noticed Samuel's left arm was in a sling. "What's the matter with your arm?"

He glanced down at the sling and gave a dismissive sniff. "Oh, that's nothing. Annie wants me to go easy on this arm until the wound in my shoulder heals. She thinks a sling will force me to not use it, and help the wound heal faster."

At the mention of Annie's name, Sarah remembered that she was supposed to seek her out about riding clothes. "Good idea. Does anyone know where she is right now?"

"She's been bustling about in the attic," the squire said. "I don't know what she's up to now."

"I'll go find out," Sarah said and left them to resume their previous conversation.

—

She located the hardworking housekeeper in her sewing room, working on a garment with her mouth full of pins. Noticing Sarah, she pulled the pins out of her mouth and smiled.

"Oh, right in time, miss. Look what I found."

She stood and shook out the garment, a lovely jade-green silk woman's riding habit with a gathered skirt and epaulets at the shoulders.

Sarah smiled at the sight of it before realizing that the garment was far too elegant for her. "It's beautiful, but don't you think it's a bit grand for me, the governess?"

"Tsk, tsk," Annie grumbled. "Your job's got nothin' to do with what you wear to ride. This one is a little out of fashion, though, so I'm takin' off some of these frills to make it a tad simpler. I think you're gonna like it when I'm done with it."

"Fine, then. Thank you so much. Where did you find it?"

Annie threw her a nervous glance, which puzzled her, then quickly looked away. "Oh, there are all kinds of old clothes in the trunks in the garret. Missus used to host a lot of fox hunts, and there was always some guest who didn't bring the right togs, so we used to keep spare things on hand."

The explanation made sense to Sarah, so she didn't pursue the matter further. "When do you think you'll be done with it?"

"Oh, next day or two."

"That's perfect. Jesse won't have me up in the saddle for several days. He wants me to do ground work first, so, no rush."

Her stomach growled, and she remembered she hadn't had much to eat that morning because she had been too anxious about her lesson. Annie heard the rumble and chuckled.

"I got some ham and biscuits down on the kitchen hearth. Why don't you go down and eat?"

Sarah smiled gratefully. "You're a wonder, Annie. I think I will."

She went back downstairs to the kitchen and found the food Annie had set aside. A kettle of water was also simmering on the grate, so she found the tea tin and made herself a strong cup to go with her lunch. She was pulling out a chair to sit down at the table when she heard a ghostly, low moan. At the sound, goose bumps instantly rose on her arms and neck.

At first, she thought it had been the legs of the chair scraping across the floor. However, she soon heard the sound again while she was standing still beside the table, and it was louder and even more doleful. Her scalp tingled and she shivered.

She froze in place, dreading hearing the sound again. When, after several moments, it didn't come, she felt as though she had imagined it after all and chided herself for being silly. She sat down at the table and picked up a biscuit sandwich, but as she did, she realized that her hands were shaking too much for her to eat it. At that moment, Annie appeared in the doorway.

"What's the matter, miss? Your face is white as a sheet."

Sarah jumped and felt even sillier. "Oh, nothing, Annie. I . . . I guess I'm becoming a bundle of nerves lately. So much has happened in the last few days, and I was nervous about my lesson this morning. Seems it's all gotten under my skin and made me a little . . . I don't know what."

"Spooky?" Annie finished the thought for her.

Recalling the ghostly sound she had heard, Sarah wished Annie had come up with another word. However, she had to admit that it fit.

"I'm afraid that's it," she said with a sigh.

Annie came beside her and put a light hand on her shoulder. "This house has been around a long time, miss. Lots of people have died here, and some say that leads to spirits in a house. I don't believe such rubbish, but some of the field hands do, and they're afraid to come around here. They say they hear and see scary things. I say they're only bein' foolish."

Sarah nodded. "I don't believe in spirits either, Annie. I'm sure that whatever I heard was simply due to my strained nerves."

Annie removed her hand and looked down at her intently. "What *did* you hear, miss?"

Sarah wished they could change the subject, but Annie persisted. Finally, she relented.

"Well . . . it was a terribly sad, moaning sound," she said, the hair on her arms beginning to rise again. "Like someone was in pain, or . . . *no*, it was more like their heart was broken. Yes, that's it. It sounded like they were in total *despair.*"

Annie looked aside, and frowned. Then she seemed to brighten.

"Oh, *that*," she said with a sniff. "Some of the help heard that before, too, and decided the hall was haunted. Turns out, it was only cats under the house growlin' at each other. I bet they've gotten back under there again."

Sarah wasn't satisfied with the explanation. The sound she had heard was nothing like the catfights she used to hear in the alley behind her boarding house back in Pittsburgh. However, she also saw that this discussion was making Annie uncomfortable, so she pretended to accept the explanation.

"Yes, that's probably what it was, Annie, cats growling at each other. How silly of me to get so rattled."

Annie's face cleared, and she was back to her usual busy self in seconds.

"You want some butter on that biscuit, miss?"

They fell into their usual, comfortable chatter, and the rest of their conversation and the day ahead was uneventful.

Over the next week, Sarah was totally absorbed in matters of horseflesh and horsemanship. Every morning, as soon as Annie could coax some food into her, she was down at the barn with Jesse and Jack; sometimes, she didn't get back to the house until supper time.

One afternoon, Annie tracked Sarah down at the barn, grumbling about having to walk her "old bones" so far. "But if I don't do that, I may never catch you long enough to get this riding habit on you. You're plum in love with this old horse, aren't you?"

Sarah laughed. "I admit I may have been a bit overzealous. It's just that I'm so comfortable down here and I enjoy all I'm learning from Jesse."

Jesse nodded. "She's a good student, Momma Annie. I think we're going to have her up in the saddle soon."

"Then you're gonna need this," Annie said and shook out the riding habit.

Sarah eyed it and thought it was still lovely, but was surprised by some of the alterations Annie had made. The most dramatic one was that she had dyed it a deep chocolate brown. She had also removed the epaulets and some of the gathering in the skirt, making it a much more simple and functional garment. Annie saw her critical gaze.

"You said you thought it was too fine for you, so I toned it down a notch or two. I thought brown suited you better, too, with your dark eyes and hair."

Sarah realized that she must appear ungrateful. "Well, it's quite the grandest gown I've ever had, so I think you made some very wise choices. I can't thank you enough."

Annie smiled with relief. "Let's duck in this tack room over here and get you in it so I can see where I need to take it in or let it out."

She shepherded Sarah into the tack room and quickly got her into the new gown. Together they ran their hands over the supple silk to settle it in place, and Sarah was pleased to see that it fit her perfectly. She also liked the faint scent of perfume that emanated from the rich cloth. She assumed that the garment had been stored with a sachet.

"You're amazing, Annie. It fits perfectly. I don't think you need to alter a thing."

"I think you're right, miss, and it does flatter you so. Makes your black eyes flash, and your white skin glow."

Sarah thought that went a bit far but thanked her nonetheless. "Well, green certainly *isn't* my color. It makes my skin look like an unripe apple."

They chuckled as they continued smoothing the folds and rechecking the fit. At last, Annie stood back, and scrutinized her work one last time.

"I think that should about do it. It's late now, and we both better get back up to the house. Why don't you leave it on and see how it feels to move about in it?"

Sarah agreed and they came out of the tack room to say good day to Jesse. When he saw Sarah, he gave a little start, then caught himself and covered it.

"Why . . . it's very becoming, miss."

"Thank you, Jesse. I like it very much myself."

A little crease came into his forehead. "It . . . reminds me of something—or someone."

Annie bustled Sarah out of the barn. "You probably remember it from some fox hunt back in the day," she mumbled over her shoulder, almost pushing Sarah ahead of her.

"What's the hurry, Annie?" Sarah asked.

"Nothin' miss. It's just that I gotta get supper on, and I've been away from the kitchen too long."

They made their way back to the house and were almost to the verandah when they noticed the squire standing at the top of the steps. He looked stricken.

"What is it?" Sarah asked, alarmed at his ashen color.

He struggled to find words. "So . . . so like *her*, it's uncanny," he finally croaked.

Sarah turned to Annie and became even more alarmed, seeing that she was fidgeting, keeping her eyes downcast, and twisting her apron in her hands. The woman was never beholden to anyone, even the master, so Sarah knew that something was seriously wrong. A frightening idea came to her.

"Annie, what have you done?" she asked in a trembling voice.

Annie wouldn't look at her.

"I don't know what you mean, miss," she said, rather unconvincingly.

Sarah had to ask the appalling question. The enormity of it made her heart race, and her head ache. "It was *hers*, wasn't it? The squire's wife."

Annie didn't reply, but continued looking away and twisting her apron. Sarah had her answer.

She glanced back at the squire and saw that he was struggling to master his feelings. She wasn't sure what those might be, but she thought she saw anger, grief, guilt, and confusion. Her heart went out to him and, despite her fears, she forced herself to go to him.

Standing before him, with the offending gown now beginning to feel like a plaster searing her skin, she struggled for words.

"I . . . I'm so *incredibly* sorry, sir. I think I know what's happened here, and I *deeply* regret that it's caused you pain. Please believe, I had no idea what Annie was doing."

He didn't answer. He probably couldn't answer, Sarah realized. She thought it best that she get out of his sight.

"I'll go and take this off, and you'll never see it again, I assure you."

She started to rush into the house, but as she passed close to him, he surprised her further when he sniffed the air. *What in the world is he doing?*

He reached out to stop her. "No, wait." He had a viselike grip on her arm, and she winced. He let go of her, and stepped back a pace.

"I'm sorry," he whispered. She was relieved that his anger was fading but deeply guilt-ridden that the grief in his face was still so strong. "It's . . . it's the first time that I've smelled her scent— since . . ." He trailed off.

"Of course," she said. "I understand completely."

"And, to be frank," he continued in a halting voice, "you look so much like her in that gown, I thought I was seeing her ghost for a moment."

Sarah shivered again, thinking there had been far too much talk about ghosts lately. She was also perplexed by the comparison he made. Eleanor Booth had been a renowned beauty—she was a plain spinster. What was he talking about? Surely, his senses were merely addled by shock.

"You were taken by surprise," she said. "It clouded your vision."

He eyed her up and down, shaking his head slightly. "No, no, it's more than that. You could *be* her right now, the same willowy figure, the same graceful posture."

She was becoming increasingly uncomfortable with the encounter and longed to escape to her rooms.

"Well, nevertheless, I'd best get out of this gown now, and see if I can help out somewhere in the house."

He scowled. "No, please. Keep the habit on. It gives me comfort to see it again."

She didn't want to agitate him further, but some intuition drove her to challenge him on this point.

"Truly, sir, I'm afraid I must insist. It wouldn't be proper to go about the house in a riding habit unless it was after a hunt. If it gives you comfort to see it, I'd be more than happy and grateful to keep it and wear it. It's a lovely garment, to be sure."

He nodded, looking a bit abashed. "Yes, yes, all right then. I'll see you at tea."

She frowned. He didn't normally take tea with her except on rare, special occasions when guests were coming. Samuel had recovered from his injury sufficiently to return to his own home, and no other guests were expected. Yet, the squire was proposing to share tea with her, alone, on the heels of this awkward, painful incident. It didn't sit well with her, although she also didn't know how to decline without making matters worse.

"Why, thank you, sir. I'd be glad to have tea with you, but I'll still go up and change out of this pretty habit."

Remembering who had made it so, she glanced back at Annie, who was still fidgeting on the garden walkway. The squire followed her gaze and seemed to remember Annie's role in the drama. He smiled dryly.

"Yes, Annie is quite the seamstress, isn't she? You're right, Miss Brinley, you should change, but please do join me in the library for tea at four o'clock. Annie, please join me there shortly yourself."

Annie looked even more nervous, but nodded, dropped a quick curtsy, and escaped to the kitchen as fast as her stout frame would allow.

Sarah seized on this opportunity to escape, too, ducked through the back door, and ran up the stairs to her rooms.

At teatime, she arrived at the library to find the doors closed and the squire's raised voice coming from within.

"It's not that I mind your finding a new purpose for Eleanor's things. In fact, when I consider the matter further, I think we should pull her whole wardrobe out of storage and give it all to charities. It's a shame to let such nice things molder in trunks somewhere. What I can't understand is why you would do such a thing without first informing me—no, more than that, without asking my permission. When was the last time I told you 'no' to anything you wanted to do? Tell me! When? I trust you implicitly, but only because I know you tell me everything. This incident puts that trust into question."

She heard Annie struggle to explain herself. "I don't know, sir. It just seemed too personal. I mean, the missus . . . her nice clothes, brought outta storage and used by someone who never even knew her. I was afraid it would hurt and upset you, which it has. Only I couldn't sort out how to bring it up to you, especially not with all the other troubles around here lately. I thought if I dyed it and changed it some, no one would notice."

There was a long pause, then Sarah hard the squire reply in a less heated tone. "Well, that helps—some. As for all we've had going on around here, you're certainly right about that. It's been chaotic lately, and you've risen to every hardship nobly. I know I couldn't have made it through the last few weeks without you, and Mr. Samuel would probably be dead if it weren't for you."

They exchanged further words in voices too low for Sarah to hear. Despite feeling embarrassed for eavesdropping, she put her ear closer to the doors.

"I think the young miss suspects, sir. She's *so* smart and notices *so* much, even if she doesn't know what it all means. She can't help but ask a whole lot of questions and put things together. The other day she heard sounds under the kitchen, and I don't think she believed the way I tried to explain it."

Sarah felt a wave of disappointment at this betrayal by a woman she had come to love and trust. Her eyes filled, but she managed to keep from spilling tears.

"Well, we'll have to warn them to maintain *total* silence in future," the squire said and then lapsed into a whisper.

Sarah had no idea what he meant by that, but decided she needed to get out of this awkward position before she was discovered or heard something else she didn't want to hear. Wiping a handkerchief over her eyes, she rapped sharply on the door. A long pause followed, and Annie opened the doors with what Sarah thought was a guilty look. If so, the squire covered for her, and came to greet her, a little too effusively, she felt.

"Welcome, Miss Brinley, right on time, as always. Please come in and have a seat by the fire. It's grown chilly these last few hours."

Sarah thought, *you have no idea how chilly*. The growing warmth she had felt for this place was gone after what she had overheard. However, she did as she was invited to do, and the squire sent Annie to fetch tea. Once the housekeeper had left, he came and stood by the fire with an elbow on the mantel, and scrutinized her face for a few moments.

"I sense some repairs might be in order. Let me endeavor to allay the apprehension I see on your face."

He paused, looking even more closely at her. "That face . . . the same oval shape, the same fine bone structure."

He caught himself and coughed into his hand. "To start with, no, I haven't lost my mind and confused you with my deceased wife. However, this afternoon for a time, the resemblance was quite startling. Furthermore, I didn't invite you to tea to make inappropriate advances of any kind. I can assure you that you can expect nothing but the most gentlemanly behavior from me at all times. I apologize for grabbing you so forcefully earlier, but as you observed at the time, I'd had a shock. I promise you, it will never happen again."

She looked up at him, trying to keep the anger and hurt she felt from showing in her eyes. "I believe you," she said with the most even tone she could muster, and he seemed reassured.

"The other thing I need to do is tender you a rather difficult, um, confession, which I hope you will keep in confidence. You've been here long enough and seen and heard enough to get a sense of how we do things on the place—what my values and principles are about how to treat our people."

There's that word "people" again, Sarah thought. *He can't be honest enough to call them what they are—slaves.* Once more, she struggled to maintain a calm face, and he continued, unaware of her feelings.

"Specifically, no one is ever beaten or whipped or punished *physically* in any way here. I won't stand for it. If an overseer breaks that rule, and they have before, they're dismissed on the spot."

He looked closely at her and seemed encouraged by her bland face.

"Having established that, surely you must understand that there are still times when some form of discipline is called for. Times when someone has done harm to his peers or to me, lied, or stolen something. On those occasions, we do have a policy of giving those wrongdoers time alone to contemplate their wrongdoing."

He glanced at her to register her reaction. She forced a curious face, and he resumed.

"So, there is a room in the kitchen root cellar where we, we . . . *put* them, for a time. Not long, mind you, maybe hours, at most a day . . . maybe two, in severe cases."

At that moment, Annie bustled into the room with Lije and the two set up the tea table. The squire took the interruption as an opportunity to enlist her help in his explanation.

"Ah, Annie, I'm so glad you've arrived to hear this. I was clarifying for Miss Brinley what she really heard from the cellar the other day."

Annie turned to him with a panicked look. He continued with a small nod in what Sarah assumed to be some kind of signal.

"*You know* . . . about how we sometimes have to discipline

ill-behaved workers by giving them some time alone in the cellar to think about what they've done? And how, naturally, they sometimes wail and whine, and consider themselves quite ill-treated. However, no one is ever deprived of food or water or chained up. Isn't that right, Annie?"

The housekeeper sighed with relief and nodded her vigorous assent to Sarah. "Yes'm, that's the truth of it. I don't know why I told you that story about catfights. Guess I thought it might upset you, to know about the . . . the . . ."

"The *reflection room*," the squire finished for her.

Annie gave him a grateful glance. "Yes'm, the reflection room, that's what we call it, all right."

Sarah weighed how to respond. She knew that this glib explanation was also a lie, although admittedly a more plausible one than what Annie previously told her. However, she still could only guess at what the truth was. Considering the possibilities, she decided that more serious punishment was probably going on than they would ever admit to.

Yet she still believed that no one at the hall was ever harmed physically. Despite her disappointment and hurt at being lied to by two people she had trusted, she also believed they were incapable of cruelty. She forced herself to at least appear to accept their story.

What else could she do? She needed this job, until she could find another one, anyway. As the prospect of job hunting occurred to her, she realized she dreaded it. After all, a part of her wanted to believe their story and stay here, to follow through on the work she had started and had loved doing—until now.

She became aware that they were both staring at her. Annie was even holding her breath.

She threw up her hands and forced a smile. "Why, of course, that explains everything. Please forgive me for being so suspicious."

They both seemed vastly relieved, and the squire hurried to her side. "On the contrary, Miss Brinley, it is I who must ask pardon for deceiving you and for making you uncomfortable by my . . . *unusual* behavior earlier. Annie here is faultless in all of this, of course, as she was only following my orders."

Annie gave him another grateful glance and seemed to find the moment a good time to make her exit. She dropped them both a quick curtsy and shooed Lije out of the room before her.

"Ring the bell if y'all need me," she called over her shoulder as she hurried away. She left the pocket doors slightly ajar so that she could hear the bell ring . . . or eavesdrop, Sarah guessed.

Maintaining her trusting act, she smiled up at the squire, thinking *now what?*

He seemed to be thinking the same thing. He stalled for several moments, went to the tea tray, and poured her a steaming cup. For a while, they avoided serious dialogue by negotiating questions about how to fill plates and whether to add sugar and cream to the tea. Eventually they ran out of diversions, and he sat down on the chaise across from her, a bit reluctantly, it seemed to her.

"So, how was your lesson today?"

She had almost forgotten. It seemed like years ago to her now, but the chance to discuss something simple and positive changed her disposition.

"It was delightful, as usual. The more time I spend with Jesse, the more amazed I am at how much he knows. The man is an equine genius."

The squire seemed equally glad to have something familiar and comfortable to discuss.

"He's a genius in other areas, as well. I believe when he's older, I'll make him my overseer. How are you and Jack getting along?"

Sarah smiled the first authentic smile since the conversation had started. "He's a darling. He was good to me from the start, but I think he truly likes and trusts me now. I'm not afraid to do anything with him anymore—clean his feet or check his teeth. What's more, he comes to the door of his stall whenever he hears me talking to Jesse and neighs 'hello' to me. Of course, the carrots and apples I bribe him with every day don't hurt, but then, when it's time to go to work, he does whatever I ask of him. Today I longed him, and worked on getting him to follow my verbal commands to change gaits. He did everything I asked of him, right away."

The squire sat back and gave her an appraising look. "It sounds like you might be a bit of an equine genius yourself, Miss Brinley."

She blushed. "Hardly that, to be sure. I do love it, though. A month ago, I thought horses were scary, stupid bundles of mindless muscle. Who would have thought that I would come to *love* them so quickly?"

He stroked his chin. "Huh. 'Scary, stupid bundles of mindless muscle.' I think you have that quite right, actually."

They both chuckled and looked down at their teacups. She realized that this change in her feelings for horses had happened only because she had come to this very special—though increasingly puzzling—place. She felt a twinge of guilt for having been so angry earlier. Although she still didn't know what to make of all the mysteries unfolding around her, she also felt the need to show her thanks for all the good she'd encountered, too.

"I . . . I'm well aware that this new appreciation—no, *love* of horses—would never had happened if you hadn't hired me in the first place and provided me all the opportunities and resources that you have here. I'm truly grateful to you for that."

He, too, smiled his first authentic smile of the evening. "It has been my pleasure, Miss Brinley."

The boyish twinkle reappeared in his eyes. "Still, remember, I'm holding you accountable for a miracle. You made a connection with my son that no one but Lije has ever been able to make before . . . you, a total stranger."

Sarah smiled, remembering that exciting day. "*Nopada,*" she said. When he looked puzzled, she translated for him. "It means 'stranger' in the boys' secret language."

"Ah," he said with a smile that registered respect and appreciation. "So, you're already learning their special words. Why didn't I think of that?"

She laughed. "Not as well, or as fast, as I'm learning about horses. Lije sits with me at breakfast every morning and gives me a few more words and phrases to memorize."

A twinkle came into her own eyes. "*Ma kekka pabada?*" she asked.

He looked at her as if she were crazy.

"More cake, please?" she translated, and after a startled pause, he burst into hearty laughter. She liked the sound of it immensely; it reminded her of her father's laugh. As he served her another piece of cake, she was glad she had decided to put the recent unpleasantness aside. She still had so much more to learn and accomplish. Whatever the challenges, she was determined to succeed.

Nevertheless, watching him across the tea table, listening to him and laughing at his stories, she realized with dismay that a huge complication was emerging. She was beginning to have romantic feelings for him.

When Sarah arrived at the stables the next morning, she was wearing the riding habit that had caused such turmoil. Jesse hadn't told that she would ride today, but she wanted to be prepared if he did. As he came out of Jack's stall, leading the big gelding beside him, he smiled to see her outfit.

"Is this a hint, miss?" he asked with his head cocked.

She blushed. "Well, you told your grandmother yesterday that you thought I'd be up in a saddle soon, so I wanted to be ready in case today was the day."

He laughed outright. "Well, if it wasn't going to be, it is now. Let's get your friend here tacked up, and we'll start you out in the small paddock."

She almost ran to him and took the lead rope out of his hands. "I'll do everything myself, and you check my work."

They cross-tied the horse in the corridor outside the tack room, and Sarah went to work putting on his bridle and the ladies' side saddle. She wished she could ride astraddle like a man, which was the way she had ridden the last time she rode as a child. However, it simply wouldn't be proper for any woman who professed herself a lady.

She pulled the saddle's girth strap as tight as she could, and Jesse came to test it.

"My word, miss, I couldn't have gotten it any tighter myself. Good work."

She beamed. "May I get on now?"

Jesse brought a mounting block out of the tack room and placed it at Jack's left side. Sarah stepped up, lifted her skirts, and, struggling to keep her petticoats from showing, placed her left foot into the lower stirrup. Using it to leverage herself up, she hopped into the padded seat and, once settled there, placed her right leg over the horn—all without any help from Jesse.

"Looks like you've been doing this every day of your life, miss," Jesse said. "Do you want me to lead you around for a bit until you get comfortable?"

"No, please, I want to do it all by myself. Just open the gate to the paddock, please."

She gathered the reins until they were the right, light tension Jesse had taught her to use and clucked. Jack took off in a stately, slow walk, his neck arched prettily and his tail raised in the air like a flag. Sarah felt so proud she could have burst the riding habit's seams.

They made their way out to the paddock, and Jesse opened and closed the gate for them. Then he jumped up on the top rail of the fence to observe her. Sarah made several walking passes around the ring, then clucked twice, and Jack broke into a gentle trot.

Slow as the gait was, Sarah found it jarring nonetheless. She remembered enjoying the rocking horse feel of the canter as a child and decided she was ready to try it. Jack had taken verbal commands well when she was working him on a line, so she simply said "canter" and the big horse broke into the gentle, rolling gait.

"Well done, miss," Jesse called from the fence top. "You look like you ride all the time."

"Thank you, I'd like to. This is wonderful!"

Eventually Jack began to lather with sweat, so she slowed him to a walk to cool him down. Finally, she knew it was time to dismount and give him a rest, but she didn't want the experience to end. Nevertheless, she led them both to the spot where Jesse was perched on the fence top and lowered the reins into her lap.

"This was the first time I've ridden since I was nine years old. How did I do?"

Jesse enthused for so long about how well she'd done that she began to feel guilty for fishing for compliments. In fact, she already knew she had done very well, but also knew that Jack was responsible for most of her success because he was such a sweet, tolerant mount. However, to have ridden a horse for the first time in years and come through the event unscathed was something she had never expected.

When they had cooled down Jack with a sponge bath and returned him to his stall, Sarah took her leave.

"What's next?" she asked before going.

He narrowed his eyes in thought. Sarah loved that pensive look he wore so often.

"I think we should keep you and Jack riding together a week or so. Then, we'll ask Lije what to do next."

It made perfect sense, as did everything Jesse proposed.

CHAPTER 12

Back at the house, Sarah couldn't contain her excitement and waltzed into the kitchen singing Stephen Foster's popular song, "The Camptown Races."

"Oh, Annie, I love horses *so*," she sighed, plopping into a chair at the kitchen table.

"That's good, miss, only don't get too comfortable there because the squire wants you to have lunch with him in the library."

Sarah wasn't comfortable with the invitation, but she didn't know how to get out of it gracefully, so she hurried up to her rooms to change.

When she arrived in the library, the squire was once again stationed at the fireplace, an elbow on the mantel. As soon as he saw her, he came to her and handed her into a chair.

"Ah, welcome, Miss Brinley. Thank you for joining me. I realize I've imposed my company on you two days in a row now, but I was so eager to hear how your first ride went."

News spreads fast around here, she thought. He had probably already heard about her success and wanted to discuss what should come next.

"It was grand," she almost crowed. "I could ride all day, every day, for the rest of my life on that wonderful horse and never tire of it."

He rubbed his hands together. "So, when do we get Benjie down to see you on horseback?"

She found the question jarring. "Oh, I don't know that we should be thinking about that yet, sir. It's early still."

He frowned. "Early? I haven't had an intelligible conversation with my son in almost a year. You've been here for weeks. How long do I have to wait?"

She understood his impatience. "I know, sir, you miss being able to talk with him terribly. All I ask is that you give us time to feel our way through this process. None of us has ever done anything like it before, and I don't want to spoil anything by moving too fast."

"I'll give you one week. One week should be enough."

"But, sir," she started, then stopped, seeing his implacable expression.

Annie and Lije arrived with the lunch tray, and she and the squire had to table their debate. By the time the servants were gone, he had moved on to other topics. Sarah listened to him politely, all the while wondering, *how am I ever going to make this happen?*

Just as Sarah and the squire finished their lunch, they heard a loud knock on the front door. When Annie opened it, a familiar voice rang out. "Where is this horseback-riding paragon whose fame is already spreading across the land?"

They heard Annie chuckle. "You are too much, Mr. Samuel. They're in the library. Can I get you a bite to eat?"

"No, thank you, I've already had lunch. May I let myself in?"

"Of course. Go right ahead."

110

He appeared in the doorway with his hat in hand and wearing a sly smile. "I never thought I'd be so happy to be back in this awful place. The last time I was here, my host almost killed me."

The squire rose to greet him. "How well I recall that night and also that, when the host couldn't manage to kill you off, you stayed for days, eating him out of house and home. I suppose you're back to clean out the rest of his larder?"

The two friends shook hands, and Samuel turned and bowed to Sarah. "Don't mind us, Miss Brinley. The better I get to know this scoundrel, the more I must work to keep him in line."

She laughed but said nothing. The squire poured Samuel a whiskey, and the two men stood at the fireplace, chatting with each other and Sarah for a few moments.

"Is this purely a social call, or is there some business reason for it?" the squire asked.

"Both," Samuel admitted. "Yesterday, Jesse brought in the load of hides from the steers you recently butchered and said you wanted them tanned with the hair intact. It struck me as odd. Did he hear you right?"

The squire seemed a little rattled by the question. He glanced at Sarah to see if she'd noticed. "Yes, as a matter of fact, he did."

"Whatever for?" Samuel asked.

The squire waved a hand at him. "Let's not bore the lady here with business matters. Why don't you stay the day, and we can come back to this discussion over cigars and brandy tonight?"

Samuel was all too pleased to oblige. He turned to Sarah. "I was on my way here when I crossed paths with the overseer, on his way into town. He told me he'd seen you riding earlier, in his words, 'Like a queen.' I had to come see for myself."

Sarah felt awkward under this spotlight. "My, there must not

111

be much news in these parts if my little horseback ride generates so much interest. However, yes, Jesse was very pleased with it . . . and I guess I was, too. I had been very nervous about it. Jack gets most of the credit, though."

"Well, I still think you deserve accolades yourself, so *brava*, Miss Brinley," Samuel said.

The squire chimed in. "What's more, now we can proceed with our plans to get Benjie to accept Miss Brinley as his companion."

Sarah stayed a few minutes longer with the men, listening to their conversation, and then asked to be excused.

"You'll join us again for dinner?" the squire asked.

"Yes, so that you can coach us out of our numerous political misconceptions," Samuel said with a wink.

Sarah glared at him but refused to bite on his hook. "Why, thank you, Squire, but I hope you'll accept my regrets. I suddenly find that I'm quite exhausted."

The truth was, she was trying to find ways to distance herself from him, as best she could anyway, in this close-knit plantation community. Her recent realization that she had romantic feelings for him had shaken her deeply.

The men were clearly disappointed but gave her their leave nonetheless. Once out of their sight, she was surprised to find herself racing upstairs to her bed, throwing herself across it, and bursting into tears.

CHAPTER 13

Sarah woke the next morning with a heavy heart. Gone was the excitement she had felt the day before over her successful first ride. Remembering the squire's mandate that she begin working with Benjie in a week, she was filled with apprehension. She could never make it happen in so short a time.

However, as she got up from her bed and began putting on her clothes, another feeling took hold of her—anger. She thought of the little boy in the room across from hers, playing and listening to his nursemaid hum happy tunes. Meanwhile, she dawdled in her room, fretting about how she was ever going to get through to him, and doubting that she ever could. She was suddenly furious with herself for being so unimaginative and timid.

He's a little boy, for heaven's sake! What is the matter with me? I'm not going to let him get the best of me just by growling and baring his teeth.

She finished dressing and strode out into the hall. She remembered the recent lesson she had learned about not letting a horse know you were afraid of it.

Maybe that will work with a raging boy, as well. But nothing ventured, nothing gained.

With her shoulders squared and her chin held high, she knocked on the nursery door, took a deep breath, and entered the sunlit room with an air of confidence she didn't really feel. In fact, her heart was beating so loudly she feared he would hear it.

As before, Benjie was standing in the middle of the room, turning in circles with his arms outstretched, chirping like a bird. At the sound of her opening the door, he stopped and whirled on her. His countenance revealed both anger at her intrusion and surprise that she would have the temerity to come into his presence again—alone this time.

She decided she wouldn't give him the opportunity to rush her again. She would take the lead. Putting up her right hand in the classic "stop" gesture, she pulled a chair from behind her, and turned it so that the back was toward him. Then she sat sideways in it, facing him over the back of the chair. If he did try to attack her again, she would at least have the barrier of the chair back between the two of them.

To her pleasant surprise, he didn't make a move toward her. In fact, he seemed startled at what she had done. He knit his brow, as if considering what to do next. Sarah took that as a good sign.

She had almost forgotten that Necie was there, and was relieved when the young woman spoke up. "Well, look here, Master Benjie. Isn't this nice? Miss Brinley's come to visit us."

Sarah glanced at her with a grateful look and realized that the wise young woman was doing some acting of her own. Necie gave her a conspiratorial smile and went to Benjie's side. Sarah realized that Necie had positioned herself to intervene should the child launch another attack.

The nursemaid continued in a soothing voice. "What should we play with Miss Brinley this morning, Benjie? Do you want to show her your toys? Or your coloring, maybe? That was a mighty pretty picture you drew the other day."

He seemed to realize what she was doing and shrugged her off. He took a tentative step toward Sarah, eyeing her speculatively. She found she wasn't concerned. Her pretense that she wasn't afraid of him had become reality. She found herself almost welcoming an encounter with him.

All right then, little man. Give it your best shot, and I'll give you my best in return. I am not afraid of you, and you are not going to get rid of me so easily.

Something about the empowered energy she was feeling must have shown in her face, for he stopped in his tracks, and stood there, eyeing her for a long while. Sarah glanced at Necie, and saw her nodding encouragement. Emboldened, she got up from her chair and walked across the room to where a collection of watercolors hung on the wall beside his bed. She let her fingers roam lightly across them and turned to him with a smile.

"My goodness, yes, these are *very* nice pictures. Why, this one of the bird looks like it's about to take off and fly away any minute."

He darted toward her, shouting, "Nopada, nopada! Namas, namas!"

To her relief, he didn't lunge at her. She wasn't truly afraid that he would. Instead, he threw himself between her and the watercolors, putting his arms up and over them so that she couldn't touch them again.

She smiled down at him and nodded. "Yes, indeed, I'm a nopada. But not namas. This nopada is *not* going away. I'm here to stay."

She gave the room a long look—taking in all the toys and paintings—to signal to him she would leave only when *she* chose. Finally, she ambled toward the door, making sure that she didn't seem in a hurry to get away from him. When she was almost there, she turned, smiled at him again, and stretched her arms out to her sides. Then turning around in circles several times, she chirped like a bird.

She stopped and sighed with pleasure. "My, that does feel rather nice. I see now why you do it."

As she left the room, she looked over her shoulder and saw Necie stifle a chuckle, while Benjie stared at her wide-eyed.

For the next few days, she continued her daily sessions with Jesse and Jack, refining her riding skills more each day. The newfound peace she felt on horseback mitigated the mounting distress she felt about the daunting task of helping Benjie recover. However, it had been why she had been hired in the first place, so she knew she had to face the challenge soon. She couldn't stall forever, riding horseback every morning. After all, she had already been there more than a month.

Too soon, the week the squire had given her was up. Sitting with Lije at breakfast when Annie was preoccupied with her cooking, she turned to him and confessed her quandary.

"What am I going to do, Lije? The squire wants me to do something. I'm out of time, and I haven't come up with a thing."

Lije, wise beyond his years, gazed up at her with somber eyes, slowly chewing a piece of bacon. "Are you a praying woman, miss?"

She hadn't expected that question and was taken aback. "Well . . . yes, yes, I am, although I have to admit I haven't put any prayer into this matter."

"Well, maybe that's what you should do, then." He smiled his wonderful smile.

Sarah felt humbled. He was right, of course. She had been too busy using her head instead of her heart, approaching this thing like some riddle to be solved. However, Benjie wasn't a clock that could be fixed by tinkering with its gears, nor was he an open, approachable child who could be cuddled and soothed out of his pain. Problems as complex as his couldn't be solved through mere reasoning. If they could have been, the squire and all his household, smart people every one of them, would have already solved them. No, the way to cure his illness wasn't a question of science, but a matter of spirit.

Annie had been right. Benjie's heart and mind had been broken by the trauma he had experienced. Sarah still didn't know how to fix them. However, something in Lije's wise eyes, and simple words inspired her. She hugged him, whispered "thank you" in his ear, and got up from the table.

Annie turned to her. "You off to the stable now?"

"Yes, I think it's time we got started."

"Have you decided what you're gonna do?"

Sarah marched out of the room with more confidence than she felt. "Why, exactly what Lije says—*pray*."

Stopping outside the kitchen to collect her thoughts, she found a quiet corner of the verandah and did indeed, pray. It felt awkward for her, and she soon realized why. She had grown up in an industrial boomtown on a small, secular college campus in an academic household. Though they had embraced a worldview that valued living in peace and harmony, her parents had not been overtly religious. There had been little mention of God and no regular prayers—not even a quick grace over their daily meals.

Her parents had gone to church primarily for friends' weddings or funerals; those, and the abolitionist meetings her father attended, which were usually held in a parish hall somewhere. As a result, she had little frame of reference for prayer.

At the same time, she had always believed in God. She had been comforted by a strong belief that a higher being watched over worldly affairs with love and compassion. Silently she prayed to that God now, putting her dilemma and fears before him and asking for answers. As she did, some measure of calm came over her.

She decided to pray to others who might be able to help her in some way . . . St. Jude, whom her childhood Catholic playmates had prayed to as the patron saint of lost causes, and her father and mother, who, having crossed over to the spirit realm, might see and know things that would be helpful to her.

Lost in her thoughts, she glanced up for a second and was startled by her reflection in a nearby window—or rather, *someone's* reflection. There, staring back at her from the glass was Eleanor—the same sweet face Sarah had seen every day in her portrait over the library mantel. Shivers went through her, and she reached out to touch the windowpane, but she found that she couldn't. Her hand was trembling too much.

She blinked several times, trying to clear the vision she knew was only her overactive imagination, but without success. It seemed to her that Eleanor was actually present there, and, to her even greater dismay, trying to speak to her. Her pretty bow-shaped mouth tried to form words, but no sound emerged. She shook her head in frustration and gave up all efforts to speak. Instead, she gazed deep into Sarah's dark eyes with a pleading look in her own lovely blue ones. Sarah gazed back, transfixed, all fears fallen away. While she didn't hear a spoken message, she knew at once with total clarity what she was going to do with Benjie.

At that moment, the beautiful face in the windowpane disappeared, and she saw her own plain countenance staring back at her.

"Thank you, Eleanor," she whispered. "I promise I won't let you down." And she turned to run to the stables.

When she arrived at the barn, she was chagrined to see that a sizable audience of stable hands and even the overseer were milling about the barnyard. The squire was smiling and chatting in their midst.

Drat the man, she thought. *Does he want to make this a circus sideshow?*

She knew that she was his employee, but she also knew that she had been commanded to make some miracle happen with Benjie today. That wasn't going to happen with them surrounded by a bunch of gawkers. The squire had ordered her to hold this event, so she decided that he needed to help her with it.

"Sir, a word," she said and gestured him aside. When they were alone, she tried to keep from raising her voice.

"All of these people have to go, *immediately*. I need to be alone with Benjie and perhaps you."

He stared at her, confused. "Why?"

"Please, just get them out of here now. They could ruin everything."

He nodded. "You seem to know exactly what you're doing, Miss Brinley. Far be it from me to get in your way. I'll clear them out at once." He went off to disperse the crowd.

Jesse was nearby and observed the interaction. He came up to her with an expectant look.

"You seem to have come up with a plan, miss."

She pulled him aside, and whispered, blushing, "I . . . I think I may have had a vision, Jesse, about what to do today. Does that sound insane?"

He stepped back and smiled. "You know what? I think you should do what your vision tells you. Just tell me how I can help."

They put their heads together and fleshed out some initial steps. By the time they were done, the squire had returned.

"All right, Miss Brinley, everyone else is gone. Now what?"

She glanced up at the house on the hill above the stables and saw to her relief that the dormer windows of Benjie's room looked down on the paddock.

"Jesse, please go up and ask Necie to make sure that Benjie looks out the window shortly. Make sure he sees all that's going on down here in the ring. Give me about fifteen minutes to saddle up and then cue her."

Jesse took off for the house. That left her and the squire alone. He still had a questioning, but also admiring, demeanor that she hadn't seen previously.

"You've never acted like this before, so . . . so confident, and decisive. I like it. I like it very much."

She felt the blood rush to her face. "Well, that's what you hired me for," she said and turned to get Jack saddled. He stopped her with a light touch on her arm.

"Tell me what to do."

She was startled. He was her employer, a slaveholder, used to issuing orders and having his will done by others. However, here he was, asking her for direction. The irony wasn't lost on her. She barely knew what she was doing herself, after all, but some spirit presence was guiding her every move.

"I'm going to ride Jack about the paddock for a while. Benjie must see me doing that from his nursery window. Jesse and Necie have that piece covered. Then, I'm going to ride Jack into the corridor of the stable. You pick up from there. Have your stallion saddled and ready to ride. Go get Benjie and have him ride behind you as you roam about the grounds for a bit. After a while, come down to the stable and ride into the corridor, too. I'll take it from there."

She could see from his expression that he wanted to ask her for explanations, but she stopped him. "Please, sir, you are going to have to trust me." He gave her a nod and left.

She leaned against the nearest stall door and whispered, "Please, God . . . and Eleanor. *Please, help us all.*"

She saddled Jack, and Jesse returned to help her mount up. Once in the saddle, she walked the horse out to the paddock and waited while Jesse opened and reclosed the gate. As she did, she looked up at the nursery window and saw two faces peering down at her.

So far, so good, she thought. Entering the workout ring, she made a gut decision to break into a canter right away. She wanted to show off her riding prowess *now.*

Jack broke into his easy lope, and she concentrated on keeping him at the same steady pace, trying not to look up at the nursery window. After several minutes cantering, she stopped him and began doing figure eights at a brisk trot. She then took him to the far end of the paddock and began doing serpentines, also at a jaunty trot.

As always, Jack performed beautifully, taking every cue she gave him without hesitation and completing his workout perfectly. She knew that this show was more about Jack's skills than hers but also knew that Benjie wouldn't know that. From this distance, all he would see was someone riding like a master horsewoman.

Looking over at Jesse, sitting at his usual post on a top rail of the paddock fence, she saw that he was grinning. He was alternating between watching her and watching the nursery window.

"He's got his eyes on you like a hawk, miss. You definitely have his attention."

"Do you think he can see who I am?"

"Not sure, miss, but he can definitely see what you're doing and that you're an excellent rider. Wait, wait. Now I see the squire behind him. They've left the window, probably on their way down here."

She glanced over at the hitching rail beside the barn door and saw that a groom had saddled and tethered the squire's big stallion. She knew that she had better get out of sight, so she went to the gate and waited while Jesse opened it.

Once inside the barn, she walked Jack up and down the corridors to cool him. She sighed with relief as she heard the squire and Benjie arrive outside, mount up, and ride off.

As she continued to cool Jack down, she passed by the tack room several times. Another idea came to her—she hoped perhaps from Eleanor, once more—and she called out to Jesse.

"Are any riding clothes stored in the tack room?"

"Yes, miss, I think so. Mainly riding hats. What do you need?"

"Can you find me a woman's riding hat, preferably one with a veil?"

Jesse darted into the tack room for several minutes. Finally, he emerged and held up a bonnet exactly like what she had ordered.

She rode over to him and put on the bonnet, arranging the veil over her face after it was in place.

"What do you think, Jesse?"

"It looks very good on you, but why cover your face?"

"I figure Benjie might take to this *nopada* better if he can't see her so well."

"Ah, good thinking," Jesse replied. Hearing hooves on the gravel drive outside, they both hurried to the dark end of the corridor. Jesse ducked into an empty stall, and Sarah waited with bated breath for the moment she had imagined, praying something good would come of it.

When the squire and Benjie appeared in the other end of the corridor, her heart began to race. He stopped his horse and turned him a bit to the side so that Benjie could see into the corridor. Once father and son were settled there, she slowly walked Jack toward them, gradually emerging into the light.

As she slowly became visible, she could see that her plan was working. Benjie stared at her with wide eyes. He raised a shaking hand and pointed to her. Then things went terribly wrong.

"Mama! Mama!" he cried. "You're back!"

Sarah reeled with conflicted feelings. She was thrilled that the boy had spoken his first real words in almost a year.

On the other hand, crushing shame seized her for fostering a lie that would surely break the boy's heart when he found it out. What had she been thinking, donning this veil? The squire

123

had mistaken her for his wife, even without her having it on. Why hadn't she foreseen that Benjie would mistake her for his mother, too?

She didn't know how, but she had to try to correct his impression. She started to lift the veil when the squire shouted, "Wait!"

Frozen, she eyed him curiously. What could he possibly be thinking? They couldn't let this poor boy suffer a single moment more under the false impression that his mother was alive. It would be unspeakably cruel.

"Come join us for a ride."

She was flabbergasted, as well as angry at the squire, and glad that the veil was there to mask her feelings. She shook her head violently, not ready to use her voice and disappoint the boy yet.

"Please?" the squire said.

"Yes, please, Mama!" Benjie called to her.

More conflicting feelings washed over her. The boy was speaking normally again, and her heart soared to hear it. However, her heart sank at the awful prospect of having to deeply hurt him soon.

She slowly walked Jack toward them. Benjie was stretching his arms out, begging to hold her. Jesse had come out of hiding and was standing nearby, waiting to see whether he was needed. The squire beckoned to him.

"Please help the boy onto the back of her saddle."

Sarah noticed that he avoided saying "my wife's saddle" or "his mother's saddle." It began to dawn on her what he was planning. Jesse did as he was instructed and lifted Benjie onto Jack, placing him on the saddle blanket behind her.

The boy put his arms around her and hugged her fiercely. She felt him burrowing his nose into the fabric of her habit, drawing in his mother's familiar scent, and another wave of shame overtook her. How were they ever going to disavow him of this lie without bringing on a relapse or perhaps even a worsening of his illness?

The squire turned his horse and clucked, and together they rode off at a leisurely walk. As they ambled along, he talked of routine matters on the plantation, what crops he'd put in, and a new brood mare he hoped to buy at the upcoming auctions. It dawned on Sarah that he was reliving a scene that must have played out countless times in his married life, and her heart went out to him. The anger she'd felt earlier evaporated in a flash.

Before, she had thought only of the boy's feelings. Now she saw how hard this must be for the squire as well and perhaps even harder, for he already knew that she wasn't his wife. He was acting this part solely to give his son a few moments of happiness, all the while knowing the child was going to be crushed shortly. How hard it must be for him to be doing something with her that he had loved doing with his wife. Sarah knew she was certainly no Eleanor. Thinking of how guilty *she* felt, she imagined how much more guilty *he* must feel.

They wandered all the way to the ferry landing at the river and stopped. The squire dismounted and came to help Benjie down. He then raised his arms to lift Sarah from her saddle, and she hesitated. They had seldom touched, and the thought of having his arms around her, even in such an innocuous way, made her tremble a bit. Nonetheless, she lifted her legs away from the saddle horn and out of the stirrup, and reached down to him.

He lifted her to the ground as if she were a piece of fluff. As he removed his muscled arms from her waist, she felt a tinge of disappointment, then embarrassment for being so silly.

125

He loosened their horses' reins so that they could graze, then motioned for her to join him and the boy. They all strolled in silence along the riverbank for a while.

As they walked, Benjie reached out to hold the hands of the adults beside him. The second his hand touched hers, Sarah felt a small jolt go through him. She looked down to try to read his expression, but saw nothing there except a small, quizzical frown. *What was he thinking, and, more importantly, feeling, right now?* She wished she could read his mind.

They wandered a winding deer path through the countless tall river birches that lined the bank. The graceful branches waved gently in the breeze coming off the water, and seemed to whisper assurances to Sarah. *All will be well. All will be well.* They soon came to a clearing with a pretty wrought iron bench in its midst, surrounded by banks of daffodils in full bloom. Watching the flowers dance in the wind, Sarah thought that this would have been a beautiful place to rest if it weren't for their present predicament.

The squire handed her into a spot on the bench, then lifted Benjie to sit beside her. In the process, the boy let go of her hand, and she noticed he didn't pick it up again once they were seated. In fact, he clasped his hands firmly in his lap, staring intently at the ground.

Sarah looked up and saw the squire gazing at the muddy currents rolling by. He looked to her as though he would rather be anywhere in the world but here, with the sad task he had before him. Then he took several deep breaths, squared his chin, and squatted in front of his son. He placed a hand on each of the boy's knees and tried to get his attention, but the boy continued staring down in silence.

Catching the squire's eyes, Sarah saw that they were shining with unshed tears. She wished she could reach out a hand to him but knew that it was both impossible and unwise. If she did, she might never want to let go again.

Clearing his throat, the squire spoke in a soft voice. "Son, I have something to tell you, something that I hope you can understand, if not now, then at least someday."

"I already know," the boy said in a hoarse whisper. Both Sarah and the squire started, peering closely at him.

"When did you realize?" the squire asked with a pained face.

"I started to know a while back when we were riding Jack together. She *looked* like Mama, and *smelled* like Mama, but after I held her a while, I knew she didn't *feel* like Mama. It was only the dress with Mama's perfume still on it. When I took her hand, I knew for sure."

"Then you know, too, that this is Miss . . ."

On an unexpected whim, Sarah butted in, "Miss *Nopada*," and raised the veil to reveal her face.

Benjie looked up at her, startled. He squinted his eyes, as if he was trying to figure her out (or read into her soul, Sarah thought). He gazed at her for a long time, then he spoke at last.

"You don't have to use the special words anymore. I don't need them now."

Sarah remembered all the hours she'd spent learning the secret language and all the anxiety she'd experienced about one day using it with her student. On another impulse, she put her hands on her hips, and feigned an indignant frown.

"What? After all that time I spent learning it, just so I could talk to you?"

The faintest hint of a smile creased the corners of his mouth.

"I knew what you were up to. I used to hear you practicing in your room. I was going to pretend I didn't know what you were saying. You were *really* bad at it, miss. Still, I couldn't believe you would do that for *me*, especially after I was so mean to you."

Sarah found herself welling up with tears and fought to staunch them. She also fought the urge to take him in her arms, for that would surely alienate him completely.

She glanced over at the squire and saw that he could no longer suppress his tears. They streamed down his cheeks onto his cravat, but he didn't move to wipe them away.

"Son, can you please believe that we didn't mean to trick you? We only hoped that if you saw Miss Brinley riding old Jack, Mama's favorite horse, you'd feel more comfortable with her. That was our only thought. Then, when you thought it was your mother, and you spoke for the first time in months, I was *so* excited, I *couldn't* break the spell—not right away, anyway."

Benjie stared at him for a long moment, then leapt into his arms, sobbing. "Papa! Papa!"

At that, Sarah gave up fighting her tears and wept openly.

The squire held his son in a tight hug. "Thank God you can cry at last. We worried so when you didn't, after the . . . afterward."

When he noticed Sarah crying, too, he reached out a hand to her. "And thank *you*, Miss Brinley. This was the miracle I asked for, and you certainly delivered it."

She wished she could leap into his arms, too. Instead, she took his outstretched hand.

"I wish I could claim the credit, but I can't. I didn't plan any of this. It simply happened, fell into place, like, like . . ."

"Like a miracle?" he said with the familiar naughty boy grin she had come to love.

They locked eyes for so long that Sarah felt she was going to drown in his and forced herself to look away. When she ventured another glance, she saw that Benjie had quieted enough to pull his face from his father's chest and wipe his nose on a sleeve. The squire took out a handkerchief and finished the job for him.

"What do you want to do now?" he asked in a tender whisper.

Benjie looked over at Sarah and back at his father. "Let's all go home."

Sarah wanted to cry again, this time for joy, but kept herself in check. They rose and started walking back to the horses. As they did, she was surprised to feel a small hand take hers, and, when she looked down, Benjie smiled up at her shyly. She thought he was the most beautiful child she'd ever seen.

CHAPTER 14

That evening in the nursery, Benjie fell asleep at last. Sarah gently extricated her hand from his, taking care to avoid waking him. He had been holding her hand, her elbow, or her skirt all day, ever since they returned from their ride by the river, as if he was afraid that she might disappear.

She didn't mind, and in fact, was thrilled that he wanted to spend so much time with her. Remembering their first encounter, she would have never dreamed such closeness with him would be possible so soon. However, somehow in the process of confusing her with his mother, then finding out the truth, it was if he had come to understand who she really was—a stranger who had arrived there out of the blue, who, for whatever reasons, cared about his welfare and wanted to help him get better.

Sarah understood that Benjie had grown up with the house staff, and they were a part of his life from his earliest memory. Though he appeared to love Necie and Annie, and they clearly loved him, she sensed that his relationship with her would be different. She had come from nowhere, solely to be with him and teach him. He didn't communicate any of this to Sarah, but she thought she could read it in his expressive blue eyes. His eyes were large and luminous, like his father's, and spoke volumes without words.

Sarah thought again about the squire's unusual behavior that day. They had returned to the house from their ride and gone straight to the library for lunch. For some reason, all of them were ravenous. She noticed that, as they ate, the squire seemed to go out of his way to catch her eye frequently and smile his thanks to her. Was there something else there, too? He was such an enigmatic man. She could never figure out what went on under that tousled mane of salt-and-pepper hair.

Now hours later, despite all there was to celebrate about this amazing day, she was glad to put it to rest. As she picked up her candlestick and tiptoed out of the nursery, she saw Necie stir on her pallet in the corner and felt comforted that the faithful nursemaid would tend to the boy's needs if he woke in the night.

She crept into the corridor, but the idea of going to her empty room just didn't feel right. She was too keyed up and restless to sleep. She decided to go down to the kitchen, find Momma Annie's tin of teas, and make a pot of soothing chamomile.

As she wound her way down the graceful walnut stairway to the second and first floors, she realized again what a simple, peaceful place River Hill Hall was. There was no grand architecture or ornamentation. By the flickering light of her candle, she saw only good solid workmanship in woods, plasterwork, and fabrics. Everywhere her eyes landed was something pleasant and comforting to see—a burnished maple highboy secretary, its pigeonholes filled with important papers; a sturdy handmade cherry settee, with one of Annie's many crocheted afghans thrown carelessly across its back; a hand-painted mural of some mythic pastoral scene; simple but clearly valuable oriental runners forming pathways amongst the burnished hardwood floors. She thought she would never tire of looking at all the beautiful, comforting things in this wonderful place.

She arrived in the kitchen, stirred the embers in the hearth to life, and soon had the teakettle simmering over the flames. Once her tea was made, she debated whether to take it up to her room or visit the library to find something to read. She did neither and wandered instead out to the verandah to take in the night air. There she found the moon burning bright.

She had just settled into a rocker when she smelled tobacco smoke and realized she wasn't alone. She peered into the darkness and saw the squire leaning against the porch rails at the end of the verandah, his face dimly lit by the moon and the ember at the end of his cigar. She felt unaccountably nervous to be alone with him here, and started to rise.

"Forgive me, sir. I didn't mean to intrude on your privacy. I'll just take my tea up to my room."

He gestured for her to resume her seat. "On the contrary. I need some company. It's a lovely night, is it not?"

She took a deep breath and nodded. "Yes, it is, sir."

"A lovely night marking the end of a momentous day," he said with a smile. He crossed the porch and took a seat in the rocker beside her. "How in the world did you ever conceive such a brilliant plan?"

She couldn't tell him the spirit of his deceased wife had inspired her, so she prevaricated.

"Well, thank you, sir, but I don't know that I'd call it 'brilliant.' I merely had a hunch and fortunately it worked."

He grunted. "Good hunch, then. I've never seen anything like it. You've a very good head on your shoulders, Miss Brinley."

She was feeling increasingly uncomfortable with this unexpected late-night encounter.

"Why, thank you again, sir. I don't know about that either. I only try to observe and assess matters and do what feels right."

"Hmmm," he grunted again, and puffed on his cigar in silence for a while.

She sipped her tea and glanced around the verandah, looking for something else to talk about. Her eyes fell on the railing and she noticed that Annie had hung another quilt there. For some reason, something about this particular one captured her attention. Finally, she figured out what it was.

"Aha!" she exclaimed and rose to inspect the quilt more closely. The squire was on his feet right away behind her.

"What is it, Miss Brinley?"

She fingered the fabric of the quilt appreciatively. Annie's needlework was so fine.

"I just figured out how Annie produces so many quilts so quickly. They're all the *same quilt*, but with new designs and symbols embroidered on the inner blocks. See how this outside border is the same blue calico and pink dimity that it always is? But the blocks in the center show wagon wheels and forest paths. Last week, they were boats and cotton bales. But why?"

The squire eyed her warily, as if trying to decide how to respond. "I'm not sure I see what you're talking about, but if you say so, Miss Brinley."

She smiled indulgently. "It's because you're a man," she said.

He smiled and moved imperceptibly closer to her. "So, you've noticed that at last, have you, Miss Brinley?"

She thought she heard a flirtatious inflection in the question, and alarms went off in her head. She moved a fraction of an inch away from him, her heart beating faster. She still had her teacup in hand and sipped it distractedly, trying to think of something to say. *What could he be thinking?*

If he noticed her discomfort, he chose to ignore it, for he moved another step toward her. Tossing his cigar butt into the yard, he leaned against the railing and crossed his arms on his chest.

"How do you always manage to be so . . . *businesslike?*" he mused. "The rare times I've invited you to tea or supper, it's almost seemed as though it pained you to accept my invitation. I've come to believe I must be quite odious."

He said the latter with a self-deprecating chuckle, but it was also clear to her that he was fishing for something. She decided it best to keep her silence, although she feared he must surely be able to hear how loudly her heart was beating.

"Ah," he said with a sigh, feigning despair. "She doesn't contradict me, thus it must be true. So I really am all that unattractive, Miss Brinley?"

She bit the hook. "Of course not, sir. It's just that . . . that I've always felt you were merely being kind, and that you couldn't truly enjoy socializing with the . . . the *help*. Besides, surely it isn't quite proper, is it?"

"Nonsense!" he exclaimed. "When I invite someone to tea, it's because I enjoy their company, nothing more. And 'not proper'? The older I get, the more impatient I become with notions of *propriety*. Women covering every inch of their bodies lest some man glimpse bare skin and be overcome with lust. What rubbish!"

She hadn't intended to anger him. However, she felt far more comfortable with his anger than she had with the covert seductive undertone of his earlier comments. She couldn't deny the irony of the situation. Here she had been avoiding him because she was attracted to him, and he believed it was because she found him unattractive.

Yet why should he care in the first place? She was his employee and, as such, clearly beneath his social strata. Why should it matter to him what she thought?

She couldn't suppress a small, bemused smile at these thoughts, and he noticed it right away. He seemed to realize he had been ranting and laughed at himself.

"Now I see. She not only finds me hideous to behold, but ridiculous as well. I suppose it's a good thing that I'm going to be away on business for a while."

Her heart sank, and she couldn't contain the sadness in her voice. "Away? On business? Where? When?"

Hearing the quake in her voice, he eyed her closely. "I leave at the end of the week . . . going out west to look into some investment opportunities. I've been putting it off for some time, wanting to see you and Benjie settled in together. Now that you are, I feel more comfortable being away for a while."

"I see," she said, fighting the unexpected urge to cry.

He moved closer to her, and when she looked up at him, he was watching her intently, a crease in his brow, with a look she couldn't quite fathom. Was it frustration? Concern?

He took a deep breath. "Will you miss me?" he asked, with a look she recognized as anxious.

Knowing full well what a terrible mistake it was, she couldn't keep from speaking the truth. "Yes, sir. I will miss you . . . *terribly.*"

He smiled with relief. "Thank the stars! Perhaps I'm not so hideous after all." He started to move even closer to her, but she held up a hand.

"Please, sir, I think you're confusing your gratitude to me for something . . . something else. I'm not sure *what*—but I can't." She turned to leave as her tears began to flow.

He detained her with a light touch. "Can't or *won't*?" he asked softly.

When she turned to him and he saw the tears and torment in her eyes, he stepped back with remorse in his face.

"Forgive me," he said. "I shouldn't have gone down this path . . . at least not now—not yet. I won't compromise you or our *professional* relationship again like this. I promise you. In addition, I believe I'll move up my plans to leave and take off tomorrow." With that, he turned and hurried down the steps into the moonlit night.

As she broke into muffled sobs, Sarah realized that within a few short hours, she had gone from one of the happiest days in her life to one of the most miserable.

CHAPTER 15

A mild June morning promised a pleasant buggy ride for the troupe of shoppers going into town for the day. Annie had complained for some time that she needed to buy new fabric and notions for fall garments, saying, "Else I'll never get things done before the chill comes on."

The squire had been out of town often recently, but on his latest return, Annie had corralled him into taking Benjie, Necie and her on a day trip to Louisville. "The boy is doing so well in his studies, he's earned a li'l fun."

Sarah watched the negotiation with the same mixture of amusement and admiration she always felt when she watched Annie get what she wanted from the squire. This time, it took little doing. Benjie was jumping up and down with excitement at the mere mention of an outing, and the squire quickly agreed.

"Good thinking, Annie. We'll shop, then take tea at Miss Jenny's Tea Room, and get the boy some of those toffees he likes so well. The park's not far from there, and he can run about and play with some other children perhaps."

Their discussion took place in the nursery. The squire liked to observe Benjie at his morning lessons whenever he was in town. Sarah did her best to seem welcoming and open to his visits. After all, he was her employer and this was his home. Yet she always felt the need to hold back some part of herself. Though he had been scrupulously polite and even cordial at times to her since their late night encounter in the spring, she knew that something significant had changed between them forever. They would never have the easy camaraderie they once did, and the loss of that pleasant rapport caused her great sadness and distress. She was embarrassed at how often it had brought her to tears.

She hung back from the discussion about the shopping trip, never expecting to be included in it, but also fearing that if she called attention to herself in any way, the squire might feel obliged to invite her. Almost as if he had read her thoughts, he glanced over at Sarah as Annie and Necie began changing Benjie's clothes.

"And what about Miss Brinley, Annie?" he asked. "Do you not think she, too, deserves a reward for all her hard work of late?"

Sarah wished it was acceptable for an employee to tell her employer to hush, and fought the blood rising to her cheeks.

"Why, yes, sir, I do," Annie said with a big smile at Sarah. "How about it, miss? All the ladies love Miss Jenny's Tea Room. The missus used to bring us sweets and little sandwiches out to the carriage whenever she went there."

She had to think fast to come up with a believable excuse. "Oh, no, thank you kindly, but I couldn't possibly today. Mr. Samuel is coming out for another lesson with Jesse, and he's asked me to join them for a ride along the river trail so that he can show me his progress."

She hoped none of them would ever check the story and learn that it was only a half-truth. For, though Samuel had indeed expressed an interest in taking a ride together some day, they had no specific plan to do so today.

"Suit yourself, miss," Annie said and returned to dressing Benjie.

Sarah squirmed under the appraising gaze the squire leveled at her. *He knows.* Hating herself for being duplicitous, she decided she would go down to the stables as soon as they left, and propose such a ride occur today after all to salve her guilty conscious.

Whatever he might have intuited about the incident, the squire accepted her story, and bid her a good ride. The travelers were soon on their way, and Sarah escaped to her room for another one of the tearful reflections she felt she was having way too often these days.

She arrived at the paddock just as Samuel was wrapping up his lesson, and she was excited to see that he did, in fact, look wonderful on horseback now. A few short weeks ago, he had bounced about in the saddle like a sack of potatoes. However, today he had excellent posture, held the reins with just the right balance of lightness and tension, and seemed happy and comfortable on horseback. Sarah approached the paddock area, and as she did, it seemed to her that he couldn't resist the impulse to crow a bit.

"So, what do you think?" he asked, as he eased his horse into a rolling canter. "Am I at *least* as skilled as the renowned equestrian, Miss Sarah Brinley, or am I perhaps, as I suspect, even a bit *more* skilled than she?"

She burst into laughter, enjoying a chance to shrug off the pervasive sadness that she felt too much lately. "Oh, without a doubt, you are far *more* skilled than she!"

He grinned broadly and grandly doffed his hat, in a movement that almost unseated him from his horse.

"Uh-oh!" he cried with a nervous chuckle. "Better stick to business here!"

Sarah joined Jesse beside his usual place on the top rail of the paddock fence, and he glanced down at her with a smile.

"He actually *is* doing very well," he said.

"I see that," she agreed. "Well enough, do you think, for us to all take a little ride along the riverbank this afternoon?"

He smiled again. "I should have seen that coming. You have your habit on, and that usually means you have a ride in mind. I do have a long chore list, but I suppose I could do a short one."

They waved at Samuel to join them in the barn, and before long, they were all tacked up, ambling down the lane to the ferry landing. Once there, Jesse started to turn them toward the birch grotto where the squire and she had sat with Benjie last spring. For some reason, Sarah felt an aversion to seeing the pretty spot just now.

"Let's go exploring, Jesse. I've never seen the river trails east of the hall, and have a fancy to check them out."

A faint shadow crossed the stable hand's face, but he soon masked it. "Last time I rode on those trails, they weren't in very good repair, miss. Besides, there's not too much to see up there anyway."

Samuel was in an expansive mood. "Let's humor the lady, Jesse. Besides, I've a mind to see what's up there, myself."

Jesse acquiesced with his usual good humor, and soon they were clopping east on one of the many winding Indian paths, once buffalo traces, which hugged the riverbank throughout the region. Sarah found the views hauntingly beautiful.

True to Jesse's assessment, the trails were wild and overgrown in many places with vines and cane. However, the thick, green canopy formed by the countless river birches that crowded the Ohio's banks made a cool and inviting haven for them. It almost seemed to Sarah like the chapel aisles of a peaceful abbey she had once visited.

However, as they continued on their way, the going got rougher and less picturesque. The terrain became more muddy and hilly, with tree-choked knolls that jutted up between the winding trails, separating them from each other. Though they could still hear each other's voices, Sarah lost sight of the two men for several anxious moments at a time. Then when they did reappear, they were farther away than ever from her. She was beginning to regret her impulsive decision to go exploring.

Jack had just finished picking his way through a dense bramble thicket when Sarah turned in her saddle to see where the others were. To her dismay, she found that she couldn't see, or even *hear* them at all. It took every ounce of her willpower not to cry out to them in fright.

"Samuel? Jesse? Are you there?" she called time and again. Finally, she heard a muffled response from Jesse.

"Yes, miss, we're here, coming up behind you. Try to stay put."

"All right," she called back, feeling better knowing her companions would be there soon. She settled into her saddle and patted Jack's neck to calm them both, then eyed the little clearing where they had come to a stop. She found that she didn't like it one bit.

The graceful birches that had whispered so soothingly were gone. The land here was crowded closely with massive sycamores that rose high into the sky, blocking out almost all sunlight. The ground was thick with undergrowth, and from the depths of that growth, she heard the sound of twigs cracking and feral animals squeaking. The smell of decaying flesh assailed her nose, and she felt sure it emanated from a small, dark cave at the edge of the clearing.

Jack, too, seemed to dislike the setting, for he began to dance nervously at the sounds coming from the undergrowth. It suddenly occurred to Sarah that there might be snakes nearby and she had always heard that horses were deathly afraid of serpents.

"Jesse, Samuel!" she called again.

"Coming!" the two men called back, and she was relieved to hear they sounded closer than they had before.

"I think I need to get Jack out of here," she cried. "I think he's smelling snakes."

After a long silence, Jesse replied. "All right then, if you must. Just give him his head, and he'll find a way out."

She let Jack's reins go slack, and, sure enough, found that the smart horse began stepping forward with slow, cautious steps. He went first one way, then another, and then stopped, sniffing the air. Sarah followed his nose, and saw a small opening in the wall of the forest in the direction he was sniffing. Taking up his reins again, she urged him toward it. When they reached the spot, he nosed his way into the foliage, and Sarah found that they were on an old Indian path once more. She breathed a sigh of relief, and clucked him into a faster walk. Before long, they were completely out of the woods, and had emerged into an abandoned pasture with signs of an old settlement at its center.

Glad to be free of the menacing forest, she let Jack roam aimlessly across the weed-grown field. Looking down at intervals as they wandered the pasture, she saw rotting timbers lying about, from old split rail fences. There had once been a farm here.

As she continued to let Jack poke about the meadow, they came upon evidence of a collapsed cabin of a substantial size. While the walls had been rough-hewn timber, they were nonetheless massive, and parts of them were still standing around the dark pit created by the collapsed roof and rotted floor of the structure. All around the limestone foundation of the cabin, she saw daylilies and daisies blooming—someone had tended this place lovingly once.

Just then, she heard the rustle of foliage behind her, and turned to see Samuel and Jesse emerging from the same exit she had used moments before. She had never been so glad to see anyone in her life.

She waited for the men to join her at the cabin ruins, and once there, they all took stock. Everyone was a bit worse for wear; all the horses had nicked their lower legs on brambles, while all the humans' clothes and hair had come awry as they worked their way through the thick forest. However, they were in high spirits to have made it through the ordeal.

As always, Samuel couldn't resist joking. "Jesse, if Miss Brinley and I ever tell you we have a mind to go exploring again, please remind us of this day, will you?"

"Yes, indeed," Sarah chimed in. "Although I'm interested to see what we've come up with here. What is this place, Jesse?"

Sarah thought she saw the glimmer of a shadow cross his face again, but he answered her matter-of-factly. "We call it the Homestead, miss. It was the old squire's first settlement here, way back when hardly any white folks lived in the region. No one's lived here or worked this land for years, though."

145

"Why not?" Samuel asked. He pointed to where his horse had pawed the ground, revealing the dark, rich loam. "It appears to be fertile soil, as good, or even better than anything at River Hill Hall."

Jesse was clearly uncomfortable. "It's an old story, Mr. Samuel—a long story. Those were different times. In those days, men were doing good just to come clear a piece of property out here, and hopefully hold onto their scalps long enough to build some kind of house and get some crops in. The lucky ones managed to bring their families along later and set up real housekeeping."

Sarah pointed. "See the remnants of old flower beds along the foundation of the house there? It looks like there was a woman's touch at least somewhere along the way."

The pained look in Jesse's eyes deepened. "Yes, miss," was all he said, which Sarah found cryptic.

"The squire's mother, I presume?" she asked.

"No, miss. The old missus never lived here."

Sarah glanced at Samuel and saw rising confusion in his face. "Then who was it?" he asked.

Jesse looked down and took a deep breath. "Her name was Immookalee. It means Tumbling Water. She came from a village at the Falls of the Ohio."

The calls of cicadas, tree frogs, and songbirds filled the long, awkward silence between them. Finally, Samuel coughed.

"Oh . . . I see," he said with a frown.

Jesse seemed to feel the need to explain things further. "No one alive today ever knew her, not even Momma Annie. The story goes that she died in a lodge she'd built out in those woods we just came through, soon after the old squire brought his missus here. Some folks say she died in childbirth. Others say she starved to death. Still others say it was heartbreak. However it happened, most folks don't like to come around here anymore—something in the air just doesn't feel right."

Sarah shivered, looked again at the abandoned flowers by the cabin walls, and imagined that heartbreak probably killed Immookalee. The pregnant silence between them lengthened until she felt the need to break it. Fortunately, her upbringing came to her rescue, reminding her that all people are equal despite the color of their skin.

"Well, as you said, Jesse, it was a different time. Who are we to question how people made their way in those days? Lots of men—and women, too—of all ages and races crossed boundaries then that polite society wouldn't approve of nowadays."

Samuel seemed to rally at this. "Exactly! Settlers have been taking native wives for centuries."

He had been trying to lessen the stigma of a white man sleeping with a native woman, but had only made matters worse. Sarah and Jesse looked quickly at each other, then looked away, embarrassed.

"Except they don't marry them," Jesse murmured. "Or the Negro women they lie with."

Samuel's jaw dropped as he realized his blunder. "I'm *so* sorry, Jesse," he said.

Ever the forgiving soul, Jesse managed a sad smile. "No worries, Mr. Samuel. Everything's good between us. But I think I've probably put off my chores long enough. We'd better get back to the hall."

He turned his horse toward the forest, but Sarah found herself balking at the idea of going back into the woods.

"Please, no, Jesse. Can't we take some other way home?"

He understood right away. "Of course, miss. I think there's probably enough left of the old drive for us to make our way out to the River Road."

She smiled in relief and the group fell into a column to leave the clearing; she brought up the rear. When the cabin was almost out of sight, she heard a loud snap, like a large limb dropping from a tree or being stepped upon by someone or *something*. She looked nervously over her shoulder, but could see nothing amiss. Still, the sudden eerie feeling that someone was there watching them persisted. Was it Immookalee, upset because strangers had disturbed the peace of her resting place and evoked her sad story? Or perhaps it was the sheriff and some of his thugs, making good on his threat to watch over the squire's doings.

The feeling got worse when they made their way out to the River Road. Sarah found that the drive to the old homestead began right in the middle of the Whipping Woods.

CHAPTER 16

Sarah scanned the shelves in the library for something that might pique Benjie's interest. He had grown bored with all the storybooks in the nursery, and by mid-August, she was eager to find some new offerings to keep him engaged in his lessons.

So far, she wasn't having much luck. She found *Children's and Household Tales* by the Brothers Grimm, the collected works of Charles Perrault, and *Fairy Tales* by Hans Christian Anderson. But these were all decidedly too grim for a child: far too many murders, mutilations, and unhappy endings. *What were the Europeans thinking?*

A muggy breeze stirred the damask draperies in the tall, open windows, and Sarah wished she could trade her stout, serviceable day dress for some lighter garment . . . until she remembered she didn't have any lighter garments, other than her nightgown. Would it be inappropriate, she wondered, to ask Annie to make her some personal garments if she compensated her for her work?

As often happened these days at the hall, she got the distinct feeling that she wasn't alone in the room. It wasn't necessarily an unpleasant feeling; on the contrary, sometimes it felt surprisingly comforting, as if someone was with her and watching out for her. On the other hand, when the feeling came to her in the kitchen or back rooms of the house, which were situated over the cellar, it caused the hair on her neck and arms to rise, and sent goose bumps all over her body.

She hadn't heard any further wailing or moaning from the cellar since spring. However, she did sometimes wake in the night and rise from her bed to see unexplained lights flickering about the property. When she asked Annie or Jesse about them, they were always dismissive.

"Probably some of the hands checking on a sick calf or ewe," they would say. But they always seemed to Sarah to rush to glib explanations that minimized her concern. Why wouldn't they at least explore the question further to make sure nothing was wrong?

Today the feeling was particularly strong, and she was embarrassed to find herself looking over her shoulder frequently. She noticed Eleanor's portrait over the mantel, and it seemed to her the beauty's eyes were indeed following her movements about the room. Frustrated with herself for being so skittish, she strode across the room to the fireplace, crossed her arms, and gazed up at the portrait with an almost defiant air.

"So, Eleanor, what is it you're trying to tell me now?" she asked aloud.

Unlike the day on the verandah when she had felt she was actually being visited and guided by Eleanor, the lips and hands in the portrait didn't move today. But as soon as she'd voiced the question, she found her eyes drawn irresistibly to the various mythological scenes on the library wallpaper, and she knew what she was being told.

"That's it," she said aloud again. Benjie was just the right age and intellect to find mythology fascinating. It had gods, monsters, and heroes and heroines fighting superhuman battles and working acts of magic . . . all the things little boys loved.

When she glanced back at the portrait of Eleanor, she couldn't help but feel that the sweet face looking down on her was particularly happy. It was almost as if the gentle eyes winked at her. Perhaps the former lady of the house had visited her, after all.

"Are you finding all you need, Miss Brinley?"

She wheeled to see the squire standing in the doorway. *He creeps about like a cat*, she thought. *How long had he been there?*

"Why . . . why, yes, sir, thank you," she stammered. "I'm sorry to startle so, but we weren't expecting you home yet."

He was obviously just in from his latest travels, still wearing dusty riding attire, and carrying a heavy mail pouch filled with correspondence.

"Nor was I expecting to be home yet, but the boat from New Orleans carried a light load and made exceptionally good time."

He started to take a step into the room, then seemed to think better of it, and stayed where he was. As always, her feelings of wanting to interact with him more warmly were mixed with her desire to insulate herself from him. The contradictory feelings left her tongue-tied like a puerile girl. He either didn't notice or pretended not to out of chivalry.

"I ran into Mr. Isaacs on the levee," he said. "I've invited him for dinner, and I hope you'll join us . . . for a change. It's a bit of a special occasion."

Her discomfort deepened as she struggled to come up with a plausible excuse to decline, but she found herself stymied.

"Thank you, sir. I'd be honored."

"Good then. Six o'clock, shall we say? That way we won't keep Annie up too late."

He nodded and was gone, but Sarah thought she saw him stifle a grin as he turned to leave.

She arrived in the formal dining room that evening to find the men already sipping bourbon, and talking excitedly.

"Is it true that she actually rode her horse up the grand staircase in the Galt House?" Samuel asked.

"Indeed it is," the squire said with an appreciative smile. "I was there and saw it myself. In those days, there was little she wouldn't do on a dare or merely to defy society's senseless rules. I wonder whether she's changed through the years."

Sarah was standing in the doorway waiting to be noticed, and tried to quell her natural curiosity, but failed. The image of a lady charging on horseback up the stairs of the elegant Galt House was just too compelling.

"Please pardon my interrupting, sir, but who in the world are you talking about?"

"Ah, welcome, Miss Brinley," the squire said, coming to take her hand and lead her into the room. At the touch of his warm palm after so many months, she realized how much she had missed him.

"We are taking about the lady reputed to be the most beautiful woman in the modern world, Mrs. Robert Hunt of New Orleans, born Miss Sally Ward, the Belle of Louisville."

Sarah didn't often read society columns, but the name registered some flicker of recognition. "Is that the woman who divorced a prominent Bostonian man because his family was too rigid?"

"Precisely," the squire replied. "And what a scandal and affront that was, a *woman* divorcing a man of such standing. He begged her to come back, but she was having none of it. What guts."

Samuel jumped in. "She's also said to wear face paint, change dresses countless times each day, and easily drink any man under the table."

Sarah wasn't sure that she found their description very admirable, but felt obliged to listen with interest as the men were so enamored of the woman.

The squire continued. "She's returning to Louisville next month to host a charity event to build a new orphanage, a musical extravaganza such as the city has never seen. It's all over the local papers today."

Samuel seemed almost transported at the prospect. "Featuring the famous Russian diva, Baroness Veleriya Verolovaya," he added proudly. Then he seemed dashed at the puzzled look on Sarah's face.

"Surely you've heard of her? She's a national heroine in my country of Belarus. As a poor, peasant girl, she single-handedly stood down a gang of the czar's Cossacks who'd come to harass the local rabbi . . . merely by singing the old Russian folk song 'Not Evening Yet' or 'The Cossack's Parable.'"

Sarah was genuinely curious. "That must have been quite a song to stand down a bunch of soldiers."

"Well, people say it was mostly her commanding voice and presence," he replied. "But the song tells the tale of a Cossack who dreams of his coming death in battle. Verolovaya reminded them of their mortality, and they withdrew. What a stroke of genius, yes?"

By that time, Annie and Jesse had appeared with serving

trays. The diners took their seats at the table, while the squire filled their wine goblets.

"How did she go from peasant girl to baroness?" Sarah asked.

Samuel warmed to his tale. "The czarina heard of her courage and brought her to the Imperial Court, where she lavished the best voice training in the world on her, and arranged an aristocratic marriage for her."

"What a remarkable life," Sarah had to admit. "It almost sounds like a fairy tale."

They filled their plates and bit into Annie's succulent pork roast, fried apples, summer squash casserole, and feather-light yeast rolls.

"Delicious, Annie, as always," the squire said and turned to his guests. "Would you like to meet the baroness?"

Samuel's eyes widened. "Do you even need to ask? I'd sell my soul for it."

Sarah smiled at his melodramatics. "I'm not sure I'd go that far. But, yes, certainly. I haven't been to a musical program in years, and never to one featuring a baroness."

"Then it's done. I have an invitation for myself plus one guest. I'll be away again that night, so you two can go in my stead and represent me."

Sarah looked across the table at Samuel and saw pink rising in his cheeks. It appeared to her that the squire was engaging in a bit of matchmaking. She thought back to their uncomfortable encounter on the verandah last spring when she'd felt he was flirting with her. If so, when she'd rebuffed him, perhaps he'd assumed it was because he was too old for her. Was he trying to pair her off with the younger Samuel now? And, if so, why would an employer care about an employee finding romance and possibly marriage? Did he still feel something more for her than he showed?

An awkward silence developed; however, Samuel's gallant manners came to the fore.

"I'd be honored to escort Miss Brinley to the program, and represent River Hill Hall for you, Benjamin."

It occurred to Sarah that Samuel wasn't worried about *how* he got to meet the legendary prima donna, as long as he *did* get to meet her. His expression for the rest of the evening was positively beatific.

Early on the morning of the musicale, Sarah carried her valise to the foyer. She was surprised to find Necie sitting on the settee, holding a large garment box across her lap and looking like an excited child.

"Good morning, Necie. What are you doing here?"

"Oh, miss, isn't it grand? Annie says the squire wants me to 'company you into town and act as your personal maid tonight! Nothing like this ever happened to me before!"

Sarah wished the squire had informed her of this plan before he set it into motion, but once more had to acknowledge that he was the master and could do as he pleased. In addition, the happy energy the young nursemaid exuded was so infectious that she couldn't help but share it. She suddenly recalled that she and Necie were about the same age, in their early twenties, and that, for the sheltered young nursemaid to get a chance to see some grand cultural event in a big, busy town must seem truly miraculous.

"Such fun we'll have," she said warmly, going to Necie and

clasping her hands. "What do you have in the box there, pray?"

Necie looked down and smiled in a conspiratorial way. "The squire says it's a secret, and not to let you open it till we get to town."

Sarah frowned. "Oh, he did, did he? And where is the squire now?"

"Oh, he's long gone, off on business somewhere this morning. Jesse's waiting out front to take us into town. We have a . . . a *suite* tonight in the Galt House, miss! Do you know what that is?"

Sarah had to laugh. "Not that I should know, never having in stayed in one myself, but it's a very grand set of rooms in an expensive hotel."

Necie looked puzzled. "But why, miss? There's just the two of us, and we fall asleep in the same room with Master Benjie all the time."

Good question, Sarah thought, but said instead, "I guess the squire wants us to have a special time for some reason. Perhaps to thank us for our work with Benjie?"

Necie looked thoughtful, then flashed a beaming smile. "Well, whatever the reason, I'm going to sleep in a *suite* tonight! I bet no other girl on this place has ever done that."

When Jesse pulled the phaeton up to one of the many carriage blocks in front of the Galt House, Sarah wasn't sure who was more excited about being there, Necie or herself. The impressive, Federal-style building was six stories tall . . . one of the tallest buildings in the city, so tall that she had to crane her neck to see the top of it.

Jesse jumped from the coach box and came to hand them down from the carriage. Glancing at other female guests disembarking from the many vehicles, Sarah was glad she didn't wear the voluminous hoop skirts that were in fashion now. She could hop down from the buggy with total ease, whereas all about her she saw other women struggling to manage the flounces and frills of their gargantuan skirts to avoid showing their undergarments, which would surely bring disgrace. The thought struck her that fashion could be such a burden for women at times . . . no, more than that, an actual form of oppression. She was glad she didn't have to worry about it, tucked away in the country, working as a governess who seldom went anywhere outside the plantation.

Jesse unloaded their bags, turned them over to a valet, and said goodbye. "Have a wonderful time, miss, and Necie. I can't wait to hear the tales you'll have to tell."

"Thank you, Jesse," Sarah replied, while Necie looked like she was going to burst with happiness.

When they entered the hotel lobby, even Sarah had to admit to being a bit overwhelmed. She had heard that the Galt House was an elegant world-class hotel—Mr. Dickens himself had said so—but she had never been in such an establishment, and she didn't really know what that meant. Now gazing all around at the impeccable classical architecture, sumptuous furnishings, and stylishly dressed guests, she had to remind herself to breathe.

The spacious area was filled with overstuffed horsehair sofas and chairs, huge potted palms, and numerous reading tables. Massive gilded columns soared into the mezzanine level above, where galleries filled with sumptuous furniture and stylish guests, looked down on the lobby below. The smell of cigar smoke, and freshly brewed coffee wafted in the breezes created by boys waving peacock-feather fans here and there. Waiters and bellhops scurried about their business, while the genteel hum of polite conversation filled the air. She had never seen, heard, or smelled anything like it.

In the midst of the opulent scene, the long grand staircase led up to the mezzanine. Sarah mused that Sally Ward must be an exceptional equestrienne indeed if she rode her horse all the way up *that* set of steps. Then she noticed Samuel at the foot of the staircase, wearing his usual white linen suit and a shy smile. She rushed across the lobby to greet him.

"It's so nice to see someone familiar in the midst of all this grandeur," she said.

He took her extended hand, and to her surprise, bent over and gave it a swift kiss. She wondered if perhaps he felt the need to be more continental in this fashionable milieu.

"It's almost tea time, and the program doesn't start until eight," he said. "Why don't you get settled into your room, and then join me down here for tea?"

"I'm famished, and I'd love to," she replied.

Samuel hailed a bellboy to help them to their room. "See you down here in a half hour," he called after them, and Sarah smiled and nodded over her shoulder.

Fortunately, their suite was on the first floor above the lobby, so they didn't have too many stairs to climb. Nevertheless, they were all breathing hard in the summer heat by the time they reached it.

When the bellhop opened the door and they first stepped into their rooms, Sarah thought there must have been some mistake. The suite was too grand for a governess and nursemaid.

"Are you certain these are the rooms Squire Benjamin Booth reserved for a Miss Sarah Brinley and her maid, Necie Booth?"

"Quite certain, miss," he assured her, and backed out of the room discreetly.

Once the door was closed, Sarah and Necie turned to each other and burst out laughing like giddy children. Together they roamed the spacious rooms, holding hands, peering into cupboards, and patting the fluffy counterpanes on the high, four-poster beds.

"I never saw anything like it," Necie said, time and again. "Do folks actually *live* like this?"

"Apparently so," Sarah said. "Though none I've ever met. Come. I have an idea. Let's go throw ourselves on this big bed and see how it feels!"

Giggling like schoolgirls, they raced to the voluminous counterpane and sunk into its fluffy depths.

By the time she joined Samuel in one of the many tea rooms off the lobby downstairs, Sarah had struck a more decorous demeanor. Still she had to smile inwardly as she thought about how much fun it had been to bounce on a bed, something she had never done even as a child. She also had to wonder why it was that she had chosen to do so today of all times? Maybe it was because she felt like she was on some kind of magical adventure.

Samuel greeted her and pulled out a chair for her. "I've taken the liberty of ordering a pot of tea and a tray."

"Wonderful! Thank you so much," she said, and filled her plate with sandwiches, while Samuel poured her tea.

"Where's Necie?" he asked.

"Up in our rooms preparing some sort of surprise for me. I don't know whether to be excited or scared."

He chuckled. "This whole jaunt is something of a surprise, wouldn't you say?"

"Indeed it is. What was the squire thinking? And our rooms! They're positively palatial! They must have cost him a fortune. But why?"

Samuel sipped his tea with a pensive face then chose his words carefully. "I get the feeling maybe he's trying to pair us off for some reason. Do you know what I mean?"

"Yes, I do. I had the very same feeling."

They both sat, sipping their tea and munching on their sandwiches in silence for a spell. Finally, Samuel spoke.

"So . . . what do you think about that?" he asked in a measured voice.

"What do I think about what?" Sarah asked, totally nonplussed. Then she realized what he meant, and was overcome with remorse as she watched his discomfiture.

"Oh, my dear, please forgive me, Samuel. I just didn't anticipate that particular question. We've been such close friends. From the moment I arrived in Louisville, I've always known that if I ever needed anything from anyone, it would be you I would turn to."

He nodded. "I feel exactly the same way."

She sat back and eyed him critically, then decided to risk a breach in manners. "You certainly are one of the handsomest men in town, there's no doubt about that. What girl wouldn't be honored to be courted by a man like you?"

He squirmed a bit in his seat. "You're too kind, and I'm flattered. But what about all the other things that we have in common . . . what we like to read, what we like to do, riding horses, walking the gardens at the hall, merely sitting and talking about everything or nothing?"

She began to see that he had given the matter considerable thought, and felt a contradictory mixture of pleasure and alarm. She remembered the day after he had been shot last spring when she had come upon him in the library with his shirt off. She had found him very attractive. There had been other times when he struck her as particularly appealing, especially when he was being playful, sensitive, or thoughtful . . . which, come to think of it, was pretty much all of the time. A surprising realization came to her. *Maybe I really could fall in love with this man . . . maybe I do already love him in some way.*

Samuel stared at her anxiously, waiting for her reply. She wished she could give him her hand in courtship. Nothing would please her more in fact. Yet something held her back, and she felt a wave a sadness wash over her as she admitted what it was . . . she was in love with the squire, hopeless though that love might be. She sighed and gave him a wistful smile.

"Yes, it's true, we do have a great deal in common, so much so that it sometimes seems we're cut out of the same cloth . . . or leather, in light of your work."

He smiled at her joke and seemed relieved to be on a lighter footing. "Do I hear a 'but' coming?" he asked softly, looking down at his lap.

She felt a stab of guilt for leaving him hanging, but also wasn't prepared to rule anything out with him. Hopeless as her love for the squire was, who knew what the future might hold? "No, not a 'but' at all, merely a 'not yet.' It's less than a year since my parents died and I'm still in mourning . . . that, and the fact that I've just started making real gains with Benjie. Those things are all I can focus on for now, but it's early still. You and I have only known each other a few months, after all. Let's see what tomorrow brings, shall we?"

He ventured a shy glance at her, and she thought she saw relief in his eyes. "As always, you make perfect sense, Miss Brinley. I thank you for not casting me away hands down. At least I have something to hope for."

She felt compelled to reach across the table and put a hand over his. "Whatever comes between us in the days to come, you are going to make some girl very happy and proud someday."

Something crossed his face . . . she wasn't sure what, but thought it was doubt.

"I hope so," he said. "But sometimes I wonder."

Sarah arrived back at her suite to find Necie almost jumping up and down with excitement over the surprise she was about to deliver.

"Oh, I can't wait another minute! Come see right away, miss."

Sarah followed her into the dressing room, and did indeed receive the surprise of her life. There on a dressmaker's form was the most beautiful evening gown she had ever seen. The dress was made of a rich sable brown silk that fell from the waist to the floor in a draped Grecian effect. The neckline and short puffed sleeves were trimmed with black onyx beads, and a pair of arm-length, white kid gloves hung over the shoulder of the stand. There, too, Sarah saw a black velvet choker to which Necie had pinned her mother's ivory cameo. The overall effect left her speechless.

Necie began to fidget. "So? *Well?* Do you like it, miss?"

"I love it, of course," Sarah said. "But I'm not sure I understand it."

Necie pulled an envelope from her pocket. "I think that's what this is for."

Sarah took the envelope from her and recognized her name in the squire's bold hand on its face. She tried to hide the fact that her hands were shaking as she opened it.

Dear Miss Brinley,

By the time you read this, I will be away on business yet again. It seems that I am away all too often these days. I grieve the time lost with my son, but take comfort in knowing that the work I am engaged in now will soon better his life; that and knowing that he is in the capable, loving hands of my family, and I consider that to include you.

For some time now, I have been seeking some way to better thank and reward you for everything you have done for all of us at the hall. I hope that you feel well paid, but money only goes so far as a show of thanks. As a result, I was pleased to find an opportunity to treat you to a special event when the invitation from Mrs. Hunt came a while ago. I know that you love the arts, but have had limited occasion to attend them due to your family's modest means, and more recently, being situated here with us out in the country, far from town. So I hope you will enjoy tonight's program, and the creature comforts of one of the best hotels in the world. Now to the hard part . . .

Some time ago, it pained me to see you for the first time in one of my wife's gowns. Since then, I have grown quite used to seeing you in that garment, and it has often given me great pleasure and comfort to know that some remnant of Eleanor still walks the earth.

Tonight I ask you the favor of wearing another one of her gowns to the musical program you will be attending. While I am sure whatever garments you have in your valise would be quite suitable for the event, I know that there will be people there tonight who are very conscious of fashion, and I would not wish for you to be outshone merely on a matter of clothes. After all, you and Samuel are representing me and my house tonight.

Admittedly, the gown is a bit dated. Eleanor last wore it when Mr. Dickens came to our home to do a night of readings in 1842. However, I believe the classic beauty and elegance of it transcends time and that when you wear it tonight, you will be one of the loveliest women in the room.

With deepest gratitude,
Your humble servant,
Benjamin Booth

Sarah didn't know whether to laugh, cry, tear the letter into pieces, or what. She had such a strange mixture of thoughts and feelings that she was mute for a time. Finally, Necie couldn't stand the silence any longer.

"What does he say?"

Sarah decided the less she said the better. "That he would be honored if I'd wear this gown that belonged to his wife tonight, since I'm representing him and the hall."

"And? You *will*, won't you?" Necie seemed unable to entertain any other possibility.

Sarah bit her lip, thinking. "I don't know. Something about

it just doesn't feel right to me. On the other hand, it's quite the prettiest gown I've ever seen."

"Well, it wouldn't hurt to at least try it on, would it?"

Sarah knew what she was doing and laughed. "If I do, I may never want to take it off again."

Necie laughed back. "Well, that was what I hoped," she admitted.

Sarah couldn't resist any longer. "Oh, well, why not?"

Together, they got Sarah out of her plain everyday dress, and soon had her in a sheer cotton shift, and then into the soft, shimmering silk. Necie fidgeted with the buttons and laces, tugging the dress here and there to get it better situated on Sarah's slender frame. Then she handed her the white kid gloves, and went to work placing the velvet choker around her neck. When she was done, she stepped back to give Sarah an appraising eye, smiling broadly.

"Oh, miss, you aren't going to believe . . ."

Sarah turned to the gilded pier glass on the wall, and caught her breath. Sure enough, it was hard to believe what she was seeing.

The rich gray-brown hue and gentle shine of the silk brought out the best in her coloring, making her skin look like fine porcelain. The black onyx beads made her black eyes sparkle, and the choker and gloves added an element of simplicity with grace.

"There's one more thing," Necie said, and approached Sarah from behind. She removed the net snood Sarah always wore to contain her hair bun. Necie fluffed out Sarah's hair, then pulled it back, and lifted it up onto the top of her head, letting several tendrils escape to fall about her neck and temples. She pulled a number of pins from her apron pocket and set the new coiffure in place with them.

Sarah had never even remotely considered herself an attractive woman, but between the gown, and the new hair treatment Necie had improvised, she felt almost beautiful for the first time in her life. Tears filled her eyes at the thought.

"Oh, Necie, *thank you*," she said, her voice thick with emotion.

Necie smiled, beginning to tear up a little bit herself. Then a mischievous look crossed her face. "All right then, miss. Time to get this gown off now, I guess?"

Sarah drew back with mock outrage. "Not on your life," she declared.

As she approached the grand staircase to descend to the lobby, Sarah felt very much like a fairy tale character . . . Cinderella attending the ball, or Sleeping Beauty awakening from her slumber. Now and then, she caught her reflection in one of the countless mirrors in the corridor, and wondered, "*Who is that lovely woman?*" Something about the gown, and the transformative power it had worked on her, made her feel like royalty, and she found herself walking with a smooth, graceful gait, almost as if she were gliding on air.

If she had harbored any doubts about her appearance, they were dispelled by Samuel's reaction when he first recognized her—or rather, didn't recognize her—at the top of the staircase. She arrived there to see him standing at the bottom of the stairs, looking more handsome than ever in black coat and tails, scanning the crowd on the mezzanine for her. She paused at the top of the stairs, looking down at him with a slight smile.

He looked right past her for several moments. Eventually, his eyes landed on her and widened. She descended the steps, still floating in her dreamlike gait, and extended her gloved hand to him when she reached the bottom step.

"Mr. Samuel Isaacs? My escort for the evening, I believe?"

He was completely bedazzled. "Sarah? Can it really be you?"

She laughed. "I certainly hope so. Though I must admit, I seem to be under some sort of charm tonight."

He grinned. "You surely are. You look absolutely . . . absolutely . . . well, words fail me. Suffice it to say, you are a *vision* tonight!"

He offered her his arm. "Would you do me the honor of sharing the evening with me, Miss Sarah Brinley of River Hill Hall?"

She looked down demurely. "Why, of course, Mr. Samuel Isaacs. It would be my great pleasure."

At that, they broke into giggles. They walked arm in arm to the salon room off the lobby where the evening's program was to be held. As soon as they entered the room, Sarah had her first pangs of doubt.

First, Mrs. Sally Ward Hunt stood beside the Baroness Verolovaya in a receiving line, greeting guests and making witty small talk with them. Sarah hadn't expected that, and something about it sent her into a panic. What would she say? What could she possibly have in common with these luminaries? She foresaw a calamity where she fumbled and inanely mumbled "how do you do" and totally disgraced the squire and River Hill Hall.

Secondly, the room was filled with women who appeared to be fabulously wealthy, with the means to garb themselves in the latest of fashions, specifically the widest and most ornately garlanded and festooned hoopskirts that Sarah had ever seen. They looked to her like a flotilla of painted carousels, bobbing and circling in a perfectly ridiculous dance. She found the skirts silly, but that didn't allay how she felt about the looks of disdain the fashionable women directed her way when she entered the hall wearing a dress that was years out of style.

Bitter tears stung Sarah's eyes, but she was determined to keep them from falling.

Samuel sensed her feelings and squeezed her arm in his. "Pay them no mind. It's jealousy, pure and simple. You're the most elegant woman in the room and compared to you, they look like a bunch of dressed up elephants."

Sarah had to laugh at that, and soon she found that she could indeed ignore the reactions of the other women. Finally, it was their turn in the receiving line, and she was surprised to find how excited she was to be announced by a footman. It added to the feeling that she was living some kind of fairy tale.

"Representing Squire Benjamin Booth of River Hill Hall, Miss Sarah Brinley and Mr. Samuel Isaacs."

Sarah and Samuel moved from the front of the line to stand before their hostesses. Sarah had to agree that Mrs. Hunt was perhaps the most beautiful woman in the world. She was somewhere in her thirties, but had the clear unlined skin of a girl, lightly dusted with rouge tonight. Her thick auburn tresses were piled high on her head and held in place by a number of jeweled combs. Her gown was a pale lilac silk that shimmered with pink and green hues in the candlelight. However, Sarah thought the greatest part of her charm was the lively light that danced in her eyes, and her low, lilting voice with a hint of a southern drawl.

The baroness spoke first. "What a fetching gown, my girl," she said.

Sarah looked and realized the baroness was wearing a dress from the same period as hers, though the baroness's dress was a rich amethyst brocade scattered with pearls. She also wore a wide diamond tiara and a necklace of jewels that completely covered her breast, but carried these treasures on her regal frame as if they were mere trinkets.

"You pay me a great compliment," the baroness continued. "Coming to my little recital here tonight wearing the fashions I feel most comfortable in myself."

Sally Ward Hunt nodded her agreement. "I've always admired a woman who had the courage to defy conventions. Your gown is quite the most beautiful one here tonight, and all the more so because it's different. Well done, Miss Brinley."

Sarah thanked her and dropped a quick curtsy, aware that Samuel was behind her and chomping at the bit to meet the baroness.

"May I introduce my escort, Mr. Samuel Isaacs, proprietor of Isaacs Tannery?"

"It's a great honor to meet you," Samuel said, and bowed with a great flourish. It was a little too long and low Sarah thought, for she saw the two women exchange amused smiles while he was bending almost to the floor.

"You're most welcome," Mrs. Hunt said, extending him a gloved hand.

The baroness eyed him speculatively. "Do I detect a slight accent in your excellent English, sir?"

He literally beamed. "You're most astute, Madam. I, too, come from Belarus."

"Ah," she replied, with a nostalgic gleam in her eyes. "Then I must sing something from our homeland for you tonight. I will take requests at the end of the program, so be thinking what you'd like to hear."

Samuel looked as if he'd died and gone to heaven. "I already know exactly what to ask for!"

Noticing the others in line behind them getting restive, Sarah gave him a gentle tug and they moved on. As they did, they heard snippets of whispers from a few women at the end of the receiving line. "Clearly a Jew . . . and in trade, at that . . . they say she's just a governess . . . and you know, Sally actually rode a horse up the stairs here!"

The gossiping women fell into malicious tittering and continued whispering behind their fans. Sarah and Samuel were both so elated simply to be at such an event that the comments didn't bother them in the least; in fact, they caught each other's eyes and chuckled.

Mrs. Hunt, however, was not so forgiving.

The footman announced, "Mrs. Jonathan Perdue, and the Misses Loretta and Lorena Perdue."

The women came forward, curtsied, and made simpering faces.

Mrs. Hunt leveled an icy gaze at them. "What a pity you disapprove of my ride up the grand staircase. I had hoped to re-enact the event tonight. Alas, I came by carriage and have no horse. Perhaps one of you ladies would like the job?"

She took the baroness by the arm and escorted her away, leaving the Perdue women sputtering and fuming. Seeing their comeuppance, Sarah and Samuel had a very hard time stifling the urge to laugh out loud.

The orchestra began tuning up, and guests hurried to find their seats. As they had planned, Necie came to bring Sarah a shoulder wrap, and then ducked behind some potted palms in a niche so that she could hear the program. The audience settled into their chairs, and were soon spellbound by one of the greatest musical talents of their time.

Later Sarah and Samuel strolled arm in arm along the promenade on the roof of the hotel, taking in the soft night air, watching the lights of the city flicker all around them, and talking excitedly about the evening's events. Normally Sarah found Samuel's tendency toward hyperbole amusing, but tonight his wildest comments about all that had happened rang true. It had definitely been a stellar occasion.

The baroness had performed a diverse repertoire of her most celebrated arias from popular operas. . . Verdi, Wagner, and Massenet . . . and had astounded the audience with her range and versatility. Then, as she'd promised Samuel, she took requests, starting with his for the Russian folk song, "Not Evening Yet." What's more, she had invited him to join her on stage and sang it to him personally, first in Russian—*Oy, te ne vecher*—then in English so that the rest of the audience could understand the lyrics. In light of the talk about an impending war, the poignant lyrics weren't lost on the audience.

Ah, it is not evening yet,
but I have taken a little nap,
and a dream came to me . . .
it was as if my raven-black horse was playing about,

dancing about, was being frisky beneath me;
. . . and there evil winds came flying out of the east,
and they ripped the black cap from that wild head of mine.
And the captain . . . was able to interpret my dream.
"Ah, it will surely come off," he said, "that wild head of yours."

Samuel was so moved that he wept openly, as did many others in the audience. Now, he seemed almost beside himself.

"Have you ever had a more spectacular evening? Has *anyone* since the dawn of time?"

Sarah smiled. "Well, I don't know about the second question, but the answer to the first one is no, I don't think I have."

"Did you see all the money people deposited in the collection trays at the end? Mrs. Hunt must have raised a fortune for the new orphanage."

"I bet you're right," Sarah agreed, suppressing a yawn.

Samuel noticed. "Ah, I'm keeping you up. Let's take one more turn and then I'll see you to your room, all right?"

Sarah nodded and they continued along the promenade.

Samuel drew a deep breath. "I wanted to thank you for what you said earlier, you know, when I asked about the possibility of us courting."

She frowned. "What did I say? I don't remember it being anything special."

"Well, for one thing, you let me down very gently, and I appreciate your leaving my male pride intact."

They both laughed at this. "For another thing, you said I'd make some girl very happy someday."

Sarah nodded. "Yes, I remember now."

"Well, that's just the thing. Sometimes . . . most times, I just can't see that happening for me."

"Why ever not, Samuel? You're very handsome, and smart, and sweet, and gentle—which is the most important thing of all. Besides, after tonight, you're going to be the man of the hour in this town. Every girl worth her salt is going to be after you."

She had meant to amuse him, but was surprised when he scowled, his face a study in inner turmoil and doubt. "I don't think so. It's just that I . . . that I . . . Oh, never mind. I'm such a coward!"

She couldn't imagine what was going on inside him, but sensed that it was some deeply personal matter he wanted to share with her, but wasn't ready to disclose yet. She gently squeezed his arm in hers.

"Samuel, whatever it is you're struggling with, please remember that I'm your true friend, and nothing could ever alter that. When and if you ever need someone to talk to, I hope you know you can count on me."

He smiled with relief and squeezed her arm back. "I think I already knew that, but thank you for saying it. Now I promised to let you get to bed after one last turn, so allow me to escort you to your room."

They slowly made their way down the floors to her suite, Sarah holding the hem of her gown up to keep from tripping on it. When they arrived at her door, Samuel turned the key in the lock and opened the door for her.

"Thank you again for being my escort, and making me the proudest man in town, having such a vision on my arm at the smartest event of the season."

To her surprise, he leaned down, placed a chaste kiss on her cheek, and then rushed out of sight down the hall.

She let her fingertips wander the place where he'd planted the kiss, shook her head with a bemused smile, and then let herself into her suite.

CHAPTER 17

Sarah finished her solitary breakfast in the kitchen, then with coffee cup in hand wandered out the kitchen door to the verandah to enjoy the newly arrived fall weather. The whole plantation was preparing for a big livestock sale. The squire was selling all of the cattle he presently had—two dozen—and he was selling them across the river, instead of in town, as usual. Even the household staff was down at the cattle barn, separating calves from their mothers, and weighing and tagging steers. When they had completed all the preparations, they would drive the herd down to the cattle pen by the ferry landing. The cattle would then be transported across the river to auction.

Sarah asked the squire why he was taking his livestock across the river to sell rather than driving them into Louisville to the meatpackers' district on Story Avenue. She was surprised by his explanation.

"I want to develop more commerce with states in the North. In case war comes, and I feel certain it will, we'll need to do business with them."

Sarah was taken aback by his lack of loyalty to the South. "Won't your neighbors take issue with that? Wouldn't it be going against Southern interests to be doing business with Northerners?"

He scoffed at the idea. "I feel no allegiance to the South, Miss Brinley, and neither, I dare say, do most people in these parts. Kentucky may be a slave state, but Louisville has always been neutral territory. The rest of the state doesn't care for us much. Mark my words, most businessmen in town will trade with whomever has the money, and that's not going to be the South. Its sole business is agriculture, and that can't go on when war is being waged across the land. The South doesn't stand a chance of winning a war with the North."

Despite being a Northerner herself, Sarah found the prospect of agriculture grinding to a halt in the South a dismal prospect. "How sad to think of all this beautiful, rich farmland lying fallow while the men who till it are off to war."

Again, the squire had little sympathy. "They will have brought it on themselves. The North doesn't want war. It's the South that's been agitating for it for years now. There's talk about secession already, all over the South. The federal government will never accept that, so they'll be forced to go to war."

Sarah saw the sense of his argument even if she didn't like the sound of it. She had let the matter drop, and they had never revisited the topic. However, since then, the squire had taken steps to develop new commerce across the river, and he seemed to be succeeding at it.

Throughout the summer, she had seen a steady stream of goods and livestock transported across the river on the ferry he owned and operated. With his biggest livestock sale yet coming up, the ferry would be in constant use throughout the day and probably even into the night.

She enjoyed seeing his excitement mount over the upcoming event. He had continued traveling a great deal, and she saw him infrequently. He remained secretive about where he traveled and why. However, whenever he did see her, and they had a few moments to talk, he was always full of plans and dreams.

She also sometimes found him eyeing her on these encounters with a look on his face that she couldn't read. There was a sadness in his eyes even when he smiled and an uncharacteristic hesitance in his speech, as if he was debating saying something, but then deciding against it. Several times when that look appeared on his face, he abruptly ended the conversation, mumbling some excuse about an errand he needed to do.

These confusing interactions troubled her, but also gave her hope that he may have deeper feelings for her. However, whenever that possibility occurred to her, she would chide herself for being foolish. She was a plain spinster who would never attract a man, especially one as dynamic and magnetic as the squire. Time to admit the awful truth and get on with her life. It was hard, though, when every time she saw him, particularly after he had been away, her heart skipped a beat.

Her best efforts to repress the deepening love she felt for him had failed and never more so than when she was listening to him share his hopes for the plantation and his son. He had announced the night before that he felt it important for Benjie to join in on this sale.

"He's going to be master here one day, so he might as well start learning the business now. Surely, he can skip school lessons for one day to get lessons of another sort. Right, Miss Brinley?"

She had acquiesced, and he had picked up Benjie and Necie that morning at dawn. On the way out the door, he'd admonished Sarah to take the day off. "Catch up on your reading of Mr. Dickens. I've just received his latest novel, *A Tale of Two Cities*, and it's his best work yet. There's a signed copy waiting for you on the library table."

She was glad of the chance for a rare sleep-in until mid-morning, followed by some even rarer privacy. It was now harvest time, and she had been at River Hill for six months. Since the breakthrough with Benjie, she had been his constant companion every day, seven days a week, from morning until night. She didn't mind, for she soon came to find him as beautiful inside as he was outside. He was a teacher's dream come true.

Now seven, he had a voracious appetite for learning. He devoured history, poetry, music, and art. His head for figures was as good as his head for the arts. At times, she felt quite inadequate to be his teacher, for, despite his young age, some days he seemed to know far more than she.

As a result, while she loved working with him, she also loved having this quiet morning all to herself. Out on the wide verandah, she sat down in one of the many rockers and breathed in the crisp autumn air. Everywhere she looked, she saw scenes of rural abundance and beauty. The vegetable patch and fields were well tended, fences and barns well painted; and the flower gardens bursting with a combination of wildflowers and Eleanor's family heirloom perennials. The beds teemed with purple coneflowers, white chrysanthemums, and tall lavender sprays of money plant, all of which Annie would soon dry for winter floral arrangements.

After a while, she noticed that Annie had hung another quilt over the railing. She went to examine it, and once more saw that the outer blocks were the same as before, various geometrical shapes in all colors and fabrics, all sewn together in a pleasing design.

However, as she'd observed to the squire last spring, the blocks in the middle of the quilts were always changing. One time, they would be embroidered with boats and wagon wheels. Another time they depicted winding trails weaving through a forest.

Today, the middle blocks of the quilt featured scenes dealing with cattle. Blocks showed cattle being herded into pens, cattle herded onto ferryboats, and still other scenes of cattle being released into open fields.

She remembered the conversation she'd had with Annie several months before about how it looked as if her quilts were telling a story or offering a map of some kind and how anxious the old woman had been about that conversation.

She also remembered a conversation last spring between Samuel and the squire. The squire had wanted some hides tanned with the hair on them, and Samuel had thought that odd. Now, looking more closely at the quilt, she couldn't figure out the connection, but she felt certain that there was one.

From her perch by the kitchen, she could look down and see the cellar door below right next to it. She noticed that the grass in front of it was trampled as if it had recently been walked on by many feet. Curious, she went down the verandah steps to the door and stared at it for several moments.

The fable of Pandora's Box came to her mind. Did she really want to open this door right now? Was it smart for her to do so? Did she have any business going down there? She knew that the answer to all of these questions was "No, of course not!" Then, she leaned down and pulled the door open anyway.

A rush of musty air blew up at her. She thought that there must be another opening to the cellar somewhere, otherwise how would she get a draft from it?

She heard something rustling in the darkness. "Hello?" she called. No one answered.

Rats, perhaps? She shuddered at the idea of running into them. Despite knowing it was crazy to do so, she gathered her skirts and stepped cautiously down the narrow stairs.

At the bottom was a sconce on the wall with a wax taper in it. She looked down at the floor and found a box of matches lying there. Lighting a taper, she surveyed the room.

It was a large space with whitewashed stone walls. The floor was hard-packed earth, and the ceiling was the underside of the thick oak slabs and massive oak beams that made up the floor of the kitchen above. There was indeed a holding pen of sorts in the corner, the "reflection room" the squire had referred to when he had described this area to her. However, it appeared to have had no recent occupants. Cobwebs hung from its bars and the plank ceiling over it.

The large room she was in appeared to have been recently occupied, and by a large number of people. Straw bedding was scattered on the floor and the smell of unwashed human bodies and Annie's cornbread and beans lingered in the moldy air.

She heard movement again and called out, "Hello?" Once more, no one answered, and gooseflesh rose on her arms.

She went to the corner of the room where she thought the sound had come from. A canvas tarp hung there. Pulling it aside, she saw a large tunnel that stretched as far as the eye could see, which wasn't far as the space was pitch black.

Again, she heard the sound of movement coming from somewhere farther down the tunnel. It suddenly occurred to her that whoever or whatever was making the sound might be coming *toward* her now. The realization threw her into a panic. Her heart raced, and her whole body trembled.

I need to get out of here, she thought and dropped the tarp back into place. Trying to keep herself from running because it seemed so undignified, she nonetheless found herself breaking into a trot back through the cellar. As she reached the foot of the steps, she looked up and saw a shadow flit across the opening above. Then, whoever the shadow belonged to slammed the cellar door closed. Sarah's panic overcame her as she heard the metal latch of the door click into place.

She fought to retain her presence of mind and resist succumbing to the terror that gripped her. Surely, someone hadn't realized she was down here. A gardener or groom had happened along and assumed the door had been left open by mistake. They had closed it, thinking they were doing a service. Yes, that must be it. Before they could walk out of earshot, she clambered up the stairs and pounded on the door.

"Please, whoever you are, there's somebody down here! There's been a mistake. Please—let me out!"

Feeling ashamed of herself for giving in to her fears, she continued pounding on the door, sounding shriller as time passed and no one came to open the door. She hated the plaintive wail of her own voice, but couldn't keep from crying out for help. She wouldn't have thought it possible for the nightmare to grow worse, but then she dropped her candle and the room plunged into darkness. She lapsed into total despair and crumpled to the floor, sobbing.

She cried for what seemed like forever and what seemed loud enough for the folks down at the cattle barn to hear. However, nobody came to the cellar door. Eventually, she found her tears subsiding, although she still felt completely helpless. Then she remembered the box of matches on the floor near where she lay. At least she could find those and the taper and bring some light back to the room. With frantic, trembling hands, she groped around and soon laid hold of both the candle and the matches. Her hands shook so badly that it took several attempts to strike a match, but she finally did. She sighed with relief as light again flickered in the dank space around her. She tucked the box of matches into her skirt pocket.

What to do now? It had been mid-morning when she came down to the cellar, and she had no idea how much time had passed. Somebody would eventually return to the house to get lunch for the workers; that is, unless Annie had packed a basket before she left that morning. Sarah could only hope not. If Annie came bustling back to her kitchen, then Sarah could pound on the plank cellar ceiling to get her attention. If not, she might be stuck here until everyone returned in the evening. Her heart sank again at the prospect, but she rallied by reminding herself that surely she wouldn't be stuck down here longer than that.

For a time, she had forgotten that she wasn't alone. When she remembered, she lapsed into a new and even greater panic. Her heart beat so hard that she thought it would burst. Climbing back to the top of the steps to get as far out of sight as possible, she huddled in a corner, praying that whoever or whatever was down here with her would leave her alone. It wasn't long before she knew that her prayer wasn't going to be answered.

Straining her ears for any sound, several times she thought she heard something, but then realized she'd imagined it when nothing materialized. Before long, though, she heard the unmistakable sound of feet shuffling toward her from deep inside the tunnel. She realized with dread that the footsteps weren't the faint, scratchy pitter-patter of animal paws. No, these were definitely human footsteps—a number of them. Not only *wasn't* she alone down here . . . she was here with a *number* of people.

With that realization, a strange thing happened to her racing heartbeat. It had been pounding hard enough to burst, but suddenly it slowed. Sarah noticed the shift immediately, feeling her pulse crawl back to a dull thud, even skipping beats now and then, and she wondered what it meant. She climbed down from her perch on the steps and walked on unsteady feet to the center of the room.

The sound of footsteps coming her way was even clearer. Her heart continued thudding in its slow, irregular way, and when she held her candle aloft to give more light to the room, she saw that her hand was no longer trembling. It was as if she were reading about her situation in a book or seeing it unfold in a play on a stage. An aura of unreality came over her, and she felt as if she were outside her body. The horror deepened when the footsteps stopped and she knew that whoever they belonged to was now on the other side of the tarp.

She listened to her heart continue to thud in its odd, slow, irregular way and wondered why. Was she developing a heart condition? She looked up at the candle she held over her head and noted that it was perfectly steady; the tremor in her hands was gone. When she looked back at the tarp, someone was lifting it aside. In the pale light of the candle, she saw a number of black shadowy figures with gleaming, white eyes staring back at her. They looked for all the world like a horde of demons. Her heart skipped several beats, then she fainted and fell to the floor.

CHAPTER 18

When Sarah came to, she was delighted to find herself riding Jack through the thick birch woods down by the river. It was a glorious autumn day, and everywhere she looked, everything was burnished in a brilliant, gold light . . . birch leaves, blades of grass, Jack's chestnut mane, even her own chocolate brown riding habit. She knew the squire was somewhere nearby, although she couldn't see him, and she was excited to think that they were both riding through the woods on their way to a rendezvous with each other.

She came to a clearing in the woods, and there he was. He had stepped down from his prancing stallion and was waiting for her with outstretched arms to catch her as she dismounted. He looked incredibly attractive and urbane to her—his thick mane of hair brushed back from his forehead, blowing in the wind; his ruddy, lined face glowing with the warmth of the day and the exertion of his ride. After he lifted her down from her saddle, he took her in his arms and carried her as a groom carries his bride over the threshold. Burrowing her face into his muscled chest, she began to wake yet again.

She was being carried in a man's strong arms, but not the squire's arms. She smelled the stale sweat of whoever was holding her and knew that it couldn't be the fastidious squire. She opened her eyes and tried to look up into the face of her—what? Rescuer? Abductor? Her heart began racing again, and she realized that her nightmare was entering another chapter. She was out of the cellar, but what new hell was she traveling through now?

She wasn't alone with this dark stranger. She heard the sounds of other people jostling around them. Smelling the damp, earthen odor in the close air around them, she realized that they must be well into the tunnel she had peered into earlier that day. It was still pitch black, but her mysterious cohort seemed to know exactly where they were going without the benefit of light. They strode confidently together through the passage as if they could see in the dark.

Eventually, though, she thought she saw a pale sliver of light shining somewhere ahead. As they continued walking, she was soon sure of it. They were coming to an opening, and her heart leapt with relief, although she still didn't know what her fate at the hands of these strangers might be. Somehow, she began to feel that they meant her no harm. If they did, they could have killed her back in the cellar without bothering to carry her all this way through the tunnel.

The opening of the tunnel drew nearer and Sarah could see faintly in the pale light. However, the group stopped right before reaching it. The man carrying her gently placed her on the earthen floor and turned to his fellows. They exchanged urgent whispers, and Sarah tried to catch some gist of what they were discussing. The best she could tell was that they had reached some critical turning point where they had to decide what to do next. As they whispered, they looked over at her now and then, and she soon came to see that they were trying to decide what to do with her.

She decided she needed to take action. She rose, dusted the dirt from her skirts, and approached the man who had carried her there. His grizzled hair and his confident manner suggested to her that he was their leader.

"Are you spokesman for your group?"

He nodded. "Yes, ma'am. You are the lady from the big boat, yes?"

So it *was* the same group of slaves. "Yes, I am," she replied with relief. "Miss Brinley, come to teach the squire's son. What may I call you?"

The big man smiled, and she was relieved to see that he appeared to be gentle. From his gray hair and the many lines on his face, she guessed him to be about Annie's age. He was probably, like the housekeeper, one of the last slaves to be transported from Africa before the transatlantic slave trade was banned in 1808.

"I am Kplorm. It means 'guide me' in Ashanti. These men here are my sons and nephews."

"Very fitting," Sarah said. "You certainly guided me well, bringing me here safely. How did you ever get away from that awful man?"

Kplorm dropped his head. "We killed him, ma'am. We had to. He was very wicked. Now we must flee to the free side of the river."

Her heart went out to them. "How can I help?"

Kplorm became agitated. "No, no, ma'am, you stay here! We have a plan. We have help."

Things she had been observing for months came back to her and fell into place. Annie had said it best. She couldn't help but watch what was going on around her and put things together.

Now, she had an idea what might be going on with these men.

"Is your plan to hide beneath cowhides and cross the river on a ferry carrying cattle?"

Kplorm narrowed his eyes and cocked his head at her. "Yes," he said cautiously.

"And someone has helped you with this plan?"

Kplorm didn't answer, but his downcast eyes told her everything she needed to know. Like a thunderbolt, everything became clear to her. The squire was operating a station for the Underground Railroad.

In her trips to the library before leaving Pittsburgh, she had learned that Louisville was a strategic Underground Railroad hub. The wailing and moans she had heard coming from the cellar under the kitchen hadn't been fighting cats *or* misbehaving slaves being disciplined. The "visitors" whom the squire told Annie about were slaves in flight. Annie's ever-changing quilts hadn't been only a pleasant pastime for her. She had a key role in the operation. Her quilts were messages to incoming slaves, telling them where to hide, and where and when to make their escapes. Exactly as Sarah had intuited, the quilts did tell a story and provided a map to weary, frightened runaways.

She had been lied to again by the same people whom she had trusted, people who had lied to her before. However, this time, she didn't feel anger or betrayal. This time, her heart soared at the revelation, and she found her eyes filling with happy tears.

She felt honored to know and be among such heroic people, people who were taking grave risks, and facing dire consequences by pursuing this moral imperative. The sheriff had said as much the night he and the bounty hunters raided the plantation.

Her tears of joy soon morphed into feelings of guilt. She had accused the squire of not considering slaves to be people, yet he had risked everything to help them. He had endured her unjust accusations and attitudes with dignity and forbearance. Her face burned with shame at the memory.

Soon another memory brought her a torrent of anxieties. The sheriff had threatened he'd find out what was going on there and that he'd be back to address it. Somebody had locked her in the cellar that morning, somebody who she now realized probably wasn't a part of the plantation. What if the sheriff or some of his bounty hunters had been snooping about the place and had locked her in the cellar to make mischief—or worse yet, set the stage for another raid?

At that thought, her heart began pounding erratically again, and she wondered once more whether she was developing a heart condition. However, this wasn't the time to worry about that. Far more urgent matters were at hand. She had to get word to the squire about what had happened to her.

"Kplorm, what is outside the opening here?"

"The cattle pen, ma'am. We wait for sundown, then put on the hides. Squire says the moon will shine tonight, but it also will rain. When the clouds come, we go out with the cattle. Then they drive us down to the river and load us onto the ferry."

Sarah had to admit it was a clever plan and one the squire had probably used frequently before. It had been months since Samuel had paid a surprise visit to the hall and quizzed the squire about why he wanted his hides cured with the hair still on them. Thinking of Samuel made her wonder whether he, too, wasn't somehow complicit in the operation, but that was another question she would have to table for now.

"Can you show me, please, Kplorm?"

The big man nodded and led her to the opening of the tunnel, situated in a little hill beside the pen. There, she looked down and saw the stack of hides waiting beside the massive timbers that held the entrance open. Covering the opening was a great pile of limbs, sapling trees, and dried stalks of the corn that had recently been harvested. She realized that it would look to the unschooled eye like a brush pile that had been dumped in the cattle pen as forage for the animals.

But, how unschooled are the sheriff's and the bounty hunters' eyes?

Peering through the brush, she saw that it was all as Kplorm had said. The cattle were milling about the pen, lowing and chewing on the brush pile now and then. Squinting, she saw Jesse and Samuel sitting and chatting on the top board of the fence around the pen. So Samuel *was* involved, after all.

She turned to Kplorm. "I need to go warn them that something might be amiss tonight."

He looked hesitant, and peered out into the pen alongside her. "Be quick and take care, ma'am. I will put the brush back behind you."

"Oh, thank you. I think I owe my life to you and your men."

He seemed embarrassed. "Please just go, ma'am, and may God go with you."

She pulled apart an opening in the brush and, taking a deep breath, wormed her way through it. Once outside, she heard Kplorm putting the brush back into place to hide the opening. For fear that they might be spied on, she worked her way along the fence line of the pen, skirting the milling animals and keeping silent until she was right on Jesse and Samuel. When she reached them, they both stared at her in shock.

"Sarah, what are *you* doing here?" Samuel asked.

Jesse nodded, frowning. "Yes, miss, this is no place for a lady, especially now."

"Shhh," she hissed. "We might have visitors. I've spent the day locked in the cellar. I've only now gotten out, thanks to Kplorm."

Again, the two men jumped. "So, you know about Kplorm," Samuel said.

Sarah wanted to fuss at him but she knew it wasn't the right time.

"Oh, you *men!* I knew months ago that something strange was going on here, but I've only now figured it out."

Samuel gave her a speculative look. "And?"

"And I'm all for it, of course."

The two men smiled with relief.

"Don't let your guard down yet," she cautioned. "Whoever locked me in that cellar this morning wasn't a member of our circle. I'm not sure who it was, but I do know it wasn't one of our own. I'm guessing it was either the sheriff or one of his bounty hunters."

Samuel and Jesse threw nervous glances over their shoulders at the surrounding birch forest.

"Where is the squire?" she asked.

"He left five minutes ago to take Momma Annie up to start dinner and give Benjie his tea," Jesse replied.

Sarah panicked again. "I don't think Annie and Benjie should go back to the house yet. Not until we figure out who locked me in the cellar and whether they're still around."

"You could catch up with them if you run real hard," Jesse suggested.

She remembered her erratic heartbeat all day. "Honestly, I'm not sure I have the energy."

Jesse's face brightened. "Or you could ride Jack to catch up with them. Mr. Samuel rode him down here, and he's tethered over there in the birch grove."

Sarah looked, saw that it was true, and her heart melted. She rushed over to the grazing horse, and pushed her face into his muscled neck, drawing in the sweet smell of his flesh. "Oh, Jack, you've come to my rescue again."

Jesse came up behind her. "Let me give you a leg up. I'll run along beside you to open up gates."

She gave him a withering look. "We don't have time to open gates. I'll have to jump the fences."

Jesse looked doubtful. "But you've never jumped, miss."

"I know," she said. "But Jack has. I think between the two of us, we can figure it out."

Jesse gave her a leg up into the saddle, an English hunt seat, and Sarah was pleased to be riding astraddle again. The folds of her full skirt fell on either side of the horse. She adjusted the stirrups, took up the reins, and turned Jack toward the hall.

"How many pastures between here and the house?"

"Two," Jesse said.

"So, I'll have to cross three fences, right?"

He nodded soberly.

She drew a deep breath, clucked twice to Jack, and the game horse broke into a fast lope. He crossed the field beside the cattle pen in twelve strides. A black four-board fence surrounded the field, and when they came to it, Sarah put her hands on each side of his big neck and leaned forward, commanding, "Jump!"

To her delight, they sailed over the fence and proceeded to cross the next field. The thought struck her that she would have loved to spend the whole day jumping if they hadn't been in the midst of a looming disaster. Jack easily took them over the next two fences, and now she could see the squire with Benjie, Annie, Lije, and Necie trudging across a newly harvested cornfield. She came upon the group and called "Whoa!" to Jack.

The squire came to Jack's side to help her down from the saddle. She struggled to keep her petticoats from showing as she threw her leg over the saddle and dropped into his arms. A flush colored her face as soon as she felt his strong hands take hold of her.

He eyed her with amusement. "It seems Jesse's riding lessons are paying off well for you, Miss Brinley. I believe you're now ready for a fox hunt."

We're facing ruin and he's making jokes, she thought, but kept her tongue for once.

"Sir, I don't think Benjie and the others should be back at the hall now."

"Pray, why?"

She motioned him aside and lowered her voice. "I spent much of the day in the cellar. Someone locked me in. At first I assumed it was one of the hands, thinking the door had been left open by mistake and trying to put things right. Now, I'm not so sure that it wasn't someone else, an intruder of some kind."

He narrowed his eyes. "And what were you doing down in the cellar, Miss Brinley?"

She blushed. "Oh, all right, I was being nosy. I saw the grass was trampled around the door and wondered why. I pulled the door open to peek inside, didn't see anything of note, so I went on down, and, and . . ."

He smiled in a forgiving way. "And then you saw a great deal of note."

She nodded, eyes downcast. He reached out and took her chin in his hand, raising it so that he could see her eyes. She was relieved to see no anger in his. She was also aware that this was the most intimate gesture he had ever extended her, and she wondered what to make of it.

"So, now you know everything," he said, and she thought she heard relief in his voice.

She gazed back at him with no shame in her eyes any more. "Perhaps not everything, but enough to know that I admire you more than ever, and also enough to believe that you, and all of us, may be in grave danger."

He nodded. "Well, if you believe so, Miss Brinley, I trust your judgment. What do you propose we do?"

"I think we should start by getting Benjie and the others off the premises. Have Jesse take them into town to Mr. Isaacs's house."

He nodded. "Good idea. Next?"

She thought she saw a gleam in his eyes and that he might be enjoying playing the role of dutiful subordinate again, but she didn't care.

"I think we should move up the plans for ferrying Kplorm and his men across the river. I think we should do it as soon as possible, moon or no moon."

He frowned. "Doesn't that raise our risk? What if someone sees well enough to detect some very strange-looking cattle in my herd?"

"Yes, yes, I know, but I don't think we have any choice. Someone is up to no good today. They may even be hiding on the grounds this very minute, possibly watching our every move and waiting for the right moment to strike."

He nodded again, gravely, then gave her his impish smile. "Are you sure you haven't spent time in the military, Miss Brinley? You could teach a course on battleground strategy."

"*Oh, you!* How can you joke at a time like this? Now, you tell me what you want me to do."

"Go with Benjie and the others, of course."

"Absolutely not," she said with a toss of her head.

"May I remind you I am your employer, Miss Brinley?"

She squared her jaw. "Not any more. I quit. And I refuse to leave, so you might as well put me to work. Otherwise I'll do as I please and probably make a muddle of things."

He shook his head, looking at her with something between frustration, amusement, and admiration.

"Oh, very well, then, Miss Brinley. You're a very obstinate woman. Go back down to the cattle pen and send Jesse here to hitch up the buggy. I'll walk the family over to the stables to meet up with him."

"And then what?"

He turned and scanned the western sky. "It's still too light to risk moving the men. Tell Samuel I want you all to hunker down in the tunnel as long as possible, then move when you think the time is right, or, rather, when you feel that you have to. We may not have the luxury of doing things when we want to tonight."

She nodded and turned to give Benjie a hug goodbye. The squire detained her, looking down on her with a face she couldn't read.

"Thank you, Miss Brinley. Not only for this latest act of service, but for everything. You have quite thoroughly changed our lives for the better. I don't know what we would have done without you."

As always when they were in proximity, she was struck by his powerful magnetism. Sometimes she wished she could leap into his arms and confess her feelings for him. But other than their confusing encounter the night after Benjie's breakthrough last spring when she had sensed that he might be flirting with her, she had no reason to believe he saw her as anything other than his son's governess. Now she was so moved by his thanking her that she didn't trust herself to speak. She simply nodded, then went to Benjie and wrapped him in her arms.

"I will see you in town shortly, young man, but don't wait up for us reading. You go to bed at a decent hour, and we'll have breakfast together in the morning."

He hugged her back without words, and, when they disengaged, gazed up into her eyes. Sarah knew exactly what he was thinking. Was this going to be another parting, another time when someone he loved and trusted disappeared from his life with no warning? She also knew she couldn't promise him anything as none of them knew how this night would turn out. Still, she thought it best to demonstrate hope and courage to him, so she put on a brave face and gestured for him to go with Annie.

That parting was even more difficult for her. The old woman peered deep into her eyes, with tears filling hers. Sarah knew that Annie, among all of them but the squire, who was a veteran of war, knew the most about facing peril and overcoming it. In Annie's loving eyes, she thought she saw the message, *"You can do this, miss."*

She couldn't stand the sadness any longer and turned to remount Jack. The squire gave her a leg up, and took her hand.

"Be careful . . . *Sarah."*

It was the first time he'd ever called her by her first name. She started a bit but also liked it. "What will you do?" she asked.

"I'm going to close this end of the tunnel so that no one ever knows it was here. I'll loosen the beams from just inside the opening, then race out before the ceiling comes down on me."

The plan sounded perilous to Sarah and she started to protest, but he shushed her.

"Trust me, it will work. I'll make my way down the tunnel to meet you all at the cattle pen. We'll close up that end of the tunnel and soon have the men on their way. Now . . . I need you to promise me something."

He squeezed her hand harder and took a deep breath. "When it's time to leave, *leave*, with or without me, but make sure you close up that end of the tunnel before you go. No one must ever know it existed, or future operations at other sites will be compromised."

"What if you haven't made it out yet? We could bury you alive."

"*No arguments, please. Do it, Sarah, for me.*" Without giving her time to respond, he slapped Jack's haunches, sending her off again for the river.

CHAPTER 19

Sarah and the others stood huddled at the opening of the tunnel, peering through gaps in the brush cover, straining their ears for any unnatural sounds. So far, all they heard were the familiar lowing of cattle and the wind soughing through the branches of the birch trees. Sarah watched their golden leaves spin through the air and rustle to the ground below, thinking how normal they looked when everything was far from normal. The soothing sounds belied the mounting tension.

The sun had set. A storm was brewing, and the moon vanished and reappeared in the gathering clouds. With luck, the clouds would eventually become thick enough to blot out all moonlight. Then, they could make their move to ferry the cattle and—more importantly, the men—across the river. If luck wasn't with them, they would have to risk being seen, in which case they hoped the hides would conceal the human cargo on the vessel.

Although they hadn't heard or seen anything out of the ordinary, Sarah was so on edge that she wanted to pull her hair and scream like a madwoman. Glancing at Samuel, she thought that he, too, looked like he wanted to jump out of his skin.

The runaway slaves seemed to be faring better than their white companions. Although clearly nervous, they all wore a look of watchful readiness. Sarah was puzzled by it at first, then she remembered that they were survivors of terrible abuse. They had overcome worse threats. They had some frame of reference for how to handle danger without succumbing to panic.

Samuel gazed up at the moon, still shining out through the clouds more than it was hiding behind them. He scowled and quoted one of Sarah's favorite lines from Shakespeare. "Oh, swear not by the moon, the inconstant moon."

"It's getting late," Sarah said. "We may have to risk crossing in spite of the moon, but *not* without the squire. We *will* wait for the squire."

She said it more to reassure herself than anything, but as soon as the words were out of her mouth, she knew that they weren't true. Samuel looked away, making her even more nervous.

"What is it, Samuel? Did he make you promise what he tried to make me promise?"

"Sarah, please . . . don't make this any harder than it already is."

Her heart fell, and she knew that the men had made a pact, that their actions for tonight had been preordained. When it was time to leave, Samuel was to knock down the support beams at the north end of the tunnel, whether the squire was there or not.

Tears filled her eyes and she couldn't speak. She turned her face away and leaned for support against one of the very beams that was soon to come down.

No, it couldn't be. They must wait for him, they would wait for him. She would make them do it.

However, she knew it was false hope. "Obstinate woman" that she was, and one who often got her way through her powers of persuasion, she also realized that she lived in a man's world. She knew that in that world, when men of good character made an oath of honor to each other, nothing could sway them from following through on it. All she could do was hope, and as the time ticked away, with no sign of the squire, she began to lose even that.

Samuel peered out through the brush cover again and sighed. "We're going to have to do something soon. I've got a bad feeling."

She paled. "What do you mean?"

He nodded his head back toward the darkness in the tunnel. "Do you smell that?"

She sniffed and noticed something she hadn't before—smoke. Instinctively, she turned to go see what was happening. Samuel stopped her, grabbing her wrist with atypical force.

"*No!* That's exactly what he forbade us doing. He made me promise we'd leave *immediately*, at the first sign of trouble, and that's what we're going to do."

"But he could be dying back there!"

"I know, and don't you think I hate it as much as you do? He's the best man I've ever known . . . the best friend I've ever had."

She saw the pain in his eyes and grieved for him. She couldn't give up on the squire, though.

"Samuel, *for the love of God*. At least let *me* go back. You don't need me. I wasn't in the plan in the first place."

Again, she saw the struggle he was going through, wanting to say yes but having to say no. He returned her pleading gaze, begging her to let it be as the squire wanted it to be.

All the fight went out of her, and she collapsed into his arms, sobbing. "No, no, no . . ."

She felt his hands stroking her hair and something soft grazing her forehead, then realized it was his lips.

"I know, I know," he murmured. "I love him, too."

She looked up at him, saw that it was true, and decided to

risk a confession, since everything was so raw and open between them now.

"I don't only *love* him," she said. "I'm *in* love with him."

Samuel looked down at her and smiled nervously. "I know. I'm *in* love with him, too."

As soon as she heard it, she realized it made perfect sense. She accepted it as matter-of-factly as if he'd disclosed he'd had toast with breakfast.

He heaved a mighty sigh. "So, given that circumstance, especially, don't you think we owe it to him to do as he wished, uh, *wishes?*"

She hated to admit it, but knew that it was the truth and nodded. She didn't think she would be able to speak for the rest of the night. They disengaged, and she noticed that the runaways were watching them with curious stares. It seemed to her as if, from their stoic perspective, they found the drama that white people engaged in puzzling.

She found Kplorm's eyes and saw wisdom and peace there that gave her heart. She dried her eyes on a sleeve and squared her shoulders.

"I guess it's time, then."

Samuel looked relieved and went to peer one last time through the brush covering.

"Finally, some good luck. The moon is completely behind the clouds. It's now or never."

The runaways donned the cowhides while Sarah and Samuel widened an opening in the brush for them to exit. When she turned again to the men, she was amazed at their transformation. Hunched over and filling the heads of the hides with their outstretched arms, they actually looked like cattle. It appeared to her that they had been practicing this performance for some time, and she felt a burst of pride for their resourcefulness. Maybe this crazy plan might succeed after all.

After checking to make sure the coast was clear, Samuel slipped through the opening and motioned for her to follow him. They circled the cattle and began prodding and shooing them closer to the hillside where the tunnel opened so that the men could slip out and merge with them less obviously. Once the herd was gathered against the opening, the men slipped out into the midst of them, blending in with them in a seamless way that Sarah never would have thought possible.

Still, she couldn't ignore the rising smell of smoke and glanced now and then toward the hall. So far, she saw nothing.

Samuel went to open the gate that led down to the dock where the ferry was waiting. Taking switches off overhanging trees, they shooed the beasts forward, swatting them now and then to keep them moving. Sarah was relieved to see that the men hidden in their midst were undetectable.

Another tense moment followed when the cattle reached the wooden dock and balked at the loud clatter of their own hooves striking the planks.

"Hah! Go, Bessie!" Samuel shouted. Despite her fears, Sarah had to smile at the sight of this soft city boy trying to play farmer. However, his tactic worked, and soon all the cattle and men were safely loaded into a pen on the wide ferry.

"Are you folks crossing, too?" Zeke asked. Even in the midst of this crisis, Sarah remembered that he was Annie's son, and how proud the old woman was of him. Somehow, just his presence gave her reassurance. If anyone could see them safely across the river tonight, it would be Zeke.

"Yes, but we need a minute," Samuel said. He came to Sarah and put a hand on each of her shoulders.

"You wait here, all right?"

"No, I'm going with you."

If the squire had even the smallest chance of making it through the tunnel to meet with them, she wanted to be there for it. Samuel nodded.

They turned to head back to the tunnel and, as they did, saw flames leaping high into the sky on the southern horizon. Sarah almost collapsed against Samuel.

"Please tell me that's one of the horse barns or hay crofts—not the hall," she said.

He sighed and stared off at the conflagration. He put his arm around her and hugged her close to his side as they walked back to the tunnel with reluctant steps. Once there, he pulled a sledge hammer from a niche inside the tunnel and hefted it over his shoulder. He turned to Sarah, and gave her a steely gaze.

"Can you make it quick?" he asked, jerking his head toward the tunnel.

"Yes, please," she said and he waved her away.

She ran farther back into the tunnel, now filled with smoke. Pulling up the hem of her dress and putting the fabric over her mouth, she ventured as far into the murky void as she could.

"Squire, are you there? Please . . . *answer me!*"

She did hear something, but it was even more disheartening— the sounds of flames crackling and burning wood hissing. If the squire had been up there, he was almost certainly dead by now. She turned, brokenhearted, and ran out of the tunnel.

"Take it down," she cried, choking and coughing, then leaned against the fence, trying to catch her breath.

Filling his lungs, Samuel swung the massive sledgehammer against one of the supporting beams. The hammer merely bounced off without having any effect. He gave Sarah a nervous glance, then swung the hammer again. Once more, nothing happened.

"Let me try the other side," he said, with an embarrassed frown.

He crossed to the other side of the opening and took a swing at that beam. Again, nothing happened. He tried, time after time, but the beam was as solid and immoveable as ever.

Sarah's face lit up. They weren't going to be able to close the tunnel opening, after all. The squire might still make his way through it to join them.

"We'll have to try something else," Samuel said. "Do you have any matches on you?"

Her spirits fell, because she knew that she did. She had pocketed them in the cellar earlier. She started to lie and say no, but then remembered that this was what the squire wanted.

With a grudging air, she fished the box out of her pocket and handed it to Samuel.

He grunted and went to work putting the brush heap back in place inside the tunnel opening. Sarah didn't have it in her to help him, no matter what the squire's wishes. She simply couldn't be a party to his demise.

When the brush was all back in place, packed inside the tunnel opening, Samuel leaned down and struck a match on his boot heel. The blue flame flared up, and he threw it into the vegetation, where it quickly caught fire. He repeated this action several times more. When he was done, a large bonfire blazed in the tunnel opening. It would not take long for the flames to become an inferno hot enough to weaken the beams and bring them crashing down. Sarah watched the fire spread in silence, tears trickling down her cheeks.

There he goes. There's no way in the world anyone could pass through that blaze and survive. Goodbye, Benjamin. I'll take care of Benjie. I promise I will.

She took Samuel's arm. "Take me away from here."

He gave one last hopeful look at the fire and sighed. "Yes, it's time."

They started across the cattle pen with slow, sad steps. As they did, they heard a new noise alongside the sound of the flames popping and snapping behind them. Sarah looked at Samuel with a question in her eyes, and he looked back at her with the same question. The sound rose to a growl and then a wild shout. They turned to the tunnel opening, now engulfed in flames. As they did, the flames parted, and a man came tumbling through them. Once outside, he rolled in the muck of the pen to smother the flames on his pants and the coat he had held over his head. As he did, he laughed like a lunatic.

They ran to him and knelt beside him, slapping him with their bare hands to help extinguish the last flames. When the fire was all out, Sarah looked across at Samuel. They were all covered in mud and manure and smelled to high heavens. However, from his loving expression, she guessed that Samuel wanted to do the same thing that she wanted to do. Together, they leaned into the squire and gently put their heads against his, sighing with relief.

Soon though, they had to get back to work. "We have to hurry," Samuel said. "Who knows where the sheriff and his men might be?"

The squire nodded. "Agreed, although I think they have their hands full right now."

"What do you mean?" Sarah asked.

He merely smiled and waved a sooty hand in the air. "I'll explain later. Right now we need to get out of here."

They helped him up, gingerly placing their hands wherever his clothes weren't burned to support him as they made their way to the ferry landing. Sarah was pleased to see the ferry was loaded with the cattle, and nowhere could she detect a man in their midst. The cowhide disguise worked perfectly.

Zeke was as relieved to see them as they were to see him. "You sure are a sight for sore eyes, sir," he said to the squire, as they all got settled on a bench in the back of the ferry.

"You too, my friend," the squire replied. "We're thankful to be in your capable hands tonight, Zeke."

No one needed to tell Zeke his business. He shoved off from the dock and soon had the craft moving slowly across the river. The rising storm hadn't broken yet, but the wind made the water turbulent, and Zeke struggled to keep them from drifting downstream.

Sarah wasn't concerned. She had confidence in the man who was Annie's only child. Her chief concern was the squire. He was sitting beside her with their bodies touching, closer than he had ever been to her. He stared north to the Indiana shore and wore an expression of powerful, mixed emotions.

She saw a deep sadness in his big, shining eyes, but also a steely resolve in the stubborn set of his jaw. She was shocked, then thrilled, then confused, when he reached over and put one of his big calloused hands over hers.

What was he intending? Was he acting merely as her employer, trying to comfort her at a dangerous, frightening time? Or was there something more to the gesture?

She looked over at him again and saw a single tear trickle down his cheek. She had never loved him more than at that moment.

A roll of thunder pulled her gaze toward the sky. She was grateful to see that thick clouds now completely obscured the moon. In fact, the only light visible was the twinkle of lamps in numerous windows across the river in New Albany—that, and the hellish glare of the blaze back at River Hill Hall.

CHAPTER 20

Sarah poured a spoonful of honey into a steaming cup of tea and handed it to the squire, who sat beside her at the breakfast table at Samuel's townhouse. He had trouble bringing it to his lips because of the bandages on his hands. Still, he insisted on doing everything for himself, despite his many burns.

The last thirty-six hours had been a whirlwind that had left Sarah's head—and heart—reeling. After crossing the river on the squire's ferry, they had seen their charges safely tucked away at the parsonage of a Methodist minister in New Albany. From there, the squire explained, the men would be escorted further north to other stations, usually by former slaves who risked their freedom and very lives to do this noble work.

Once the group had seen the men to safety, they had traveled by a hackney cab east to Jeffersonville and ferried back across the river into sleeping downtown Louisville. Under cloak of darkness, they had made their way to Samuel's townhouse, situated next to his tannery in the heart of the business district on Market Street.

A joyful, albeit tearful, reunion followed with Benjie, who had insisted on staying up to wait for them. Annie, Jesse, Lije, and Necie were there, too, and everyone joined in the celebration. However, Annie first saw to it that they all had baths to wash away the muck from the cattle pen. Next, she did her best to treat the squire's burns, all the while lamenting that she didn't have her medicine bag. Once that was taken care of, the group talked the night away and slept in late the next morning.

They all rested most of the next day and gathered their strength. By the following morning, they were ready to take next steps. Over breakfast with Sarah and Samuel, the squire announced that they would not return to live at the plantation. In response to their dismayed questions, he merely smiled mysteriously and promised explanations later.

He also said that he had sent a message to his attorney, commissioning the man to begin the complex business of finding safe homes north of the river for all of his Negroes. The task was challenging, especially since it all had to be done under the strictest confidentiality.

Listening to him talk, Sarah felt greatly relieved and blessed to be sitting at a sunlit table with loved ones sharing breakfast. *I didn't know scrambled eggs could taste so good*, she mused.

A copy of the morning paper lay open before Samuel, who read the headlines aloud with malicious mirth.

"Beloved Local Landowner Feared Dead in Tragic House Fire."

The article described how the county sheriff, on a "routine patrol" at sundown two nights previously noticed smoke coming from the vicinity of River Hill Hall. According to him, by the time he and the group of deputies who were accompanying him reached the residence, it was engulfed in flames. The sheriff and his men "tried valiantly" to see if anyone was inside the home but were beaten back by the intensity of the blaze. The article concluded that when the site cooled sufficiently for a search through the rubble, an investigation would proceed as to the cause of the fire and the fate of the hall's owner and his family.

The squire exploded. "What rubbish! The man came to the front door, uninvited as before, and pounded on it, saying he had a search warrant now, so I could go to the devil."

"I presume the 'deputies' were his mongrel pack of bounty hunters?" Samuel asked.

"Of course, and from the way they were all stumbling about, I'm sure they were stinking drunk."

"I do like the way they've lionized you here so nobly," Samuel said. "*Beloved local landowner* . . . I wonder where they heard *that*? They certainly didn't interview *me*."

"That's enough out of you," the squire growled, but Sarah saw that they were enjoying their old sparring games again. Thinking of how close they had all come to losing each other, she teared up.

"What is it, Sarah?" the squire asked. She was glad that he had continued calling her by her first name.

She smiled. "Why, you two, of course. I didn't realize until now how much I enjoy your going at each other. It's quite as entertaining as anything by Mr. Dickens."

Benjie and a litter of terrier puppies came bounding into the breakfast room. Without permission or hesitation, he climbed into Sarah's lap and began pilfering her leftover popovers. Annie and Necie were hot on his trail, chiding him. "You're too big now to sit on Miss Sarah's lap. Leave the grownups alone." However, he was having none of that, and neither was the squire.

"Let him be, Annie. Looks to me like he's not squashed Sarah yet, and he's certainly not bothering Samuel or me."

"No, indeed," Sarah agreed, putting her arms around the boy and squeezing him tight.

The women went off to the kitchen where Annie was renewing an old rivalry with the Isaacs's cook, Daisy. The two had sparred for years as happily as their masters did, and Annie was eager to get back to the latest debate concerning who made the lightest dumplings.

Samuel nodded toward Benjie. "Perhaps we should table the discussion we were pursuing?"

"I don't see why," the squire said. "He's as bright as any of us here, and I want him to know early what perfidy some of our local officials perpetrate."

"What's perfidy, Papa?" Benjie asked, around a mouthful of popover.

"Treachery," the squire said grimly. "The purposeful breaking of a trust or promise."

"Oh." The boy shrugged and slid off Sarah's lap to resume playing with the puppies on the floor.

Samuel scowled. "Well, that aptly describes our sheriff and his merry band of ghouls. I'm starting a campaign to have him ousted from office next election."

Despite her joy that they were all still alive, and more than that, together, Sarah nonetheless mourned the loss of River Hill Hall. It was a place where she had been happier, and, at times, sadder, than ever before. It had etched a special place in her heart.

"Squire, um, *Benjamin*," she began, deciding to risk addressing him by his first name. "I still don't understand how the hall burned down. What happened?"

A pained look crossed his face, and she was sorry to have troubled him with her question. However, he answered with equanimity.

"I wasn't about to let those thugs ransack my home. I'd rather burn it to the ground myself than let them violate Eleanor's beautiful things with their filthy hands. So I shouted back through the door, 'You have a search warrant? Fine, search this!' Then, I went through every room on the first floor, lit the glass oil lamps, and shattered them against the walls. I *had* to divert them from things going on down at the ferry. It appears I succeeded."

Sarah teared up again at the thought of him feeling he had no choice but to destroy something he loved almost as much as any family member or friend. As he continued, she reached across the table and lightly touched a fingertip to his bandaged hands.

"The fire grew so hot, so fast, that I barely made it to the cellar to knock out the beams to the tunnel."

"And how *did* you do that? Samuel asked with a loaded look at Sarah.

"Turns out, I couldn't. They were simply too stout."

"Aha!" Samuel crowed, and the squire eyed him curiously. Sarah understood, though, and leaned closer to him.

"It's a long story. I'll tell you later."

"Anyway, by the way the fire was taking off upstairs, I figured it would burn through the beams eventually, so I let them be. I began making my way out the tunnel, but the smoke got so thick, I was almost overcome. The last bit of the journey I was crawling on my belly. I heard you calling to me, Sarah, but was too weak to answer. I was doing good just to keep moving, although I will say hearing your voice gave me the courage I needed to keep going. Once I reached the end, I somehow rallied enough strength— and anger—to stand up, and charge through that wall of flame. By the way, thank you both for doing as I asked and setting that fire to close up the tunnel."

Sarah's hand went to her throat. "Oh, my God. I'm so glad we delayed as long as we did. If we had done it even a minute or two earlier, you'd surely be dead."

Samuel winked at her and turned to the squire. "Be thankful for stubborn women, my friend. It took me forever to get her to agree to your wishes, and she's right. If we hadn't been locked in battle over the matter for so long, you would indeed be dead."

The squire gazed at Sarah with an adoring expression—one she had longed to see, but never expected, since she first realized she was falling in love with him. He didn't say anything in words, but he didn't need to.

Samuel seemed determined to play the pragmatic problem-solver. Sarah guessed it was because he was still smarting from lacking the physical prowess to fell the beams the other night. "I love the fact that the sheriff is sweating whether you're dead and worried that he might be found responsible if you are. But how long are you going to let him squirm?"

The squire sighed. "I've been thinking about that. The longer the runaways have, the farther north they can get. The Fugitive Slave Act made it legal for owners to track them down even in freed states. Thankfully, few owners want to go to the trouble or expense to travel very far. If our friends can make it well north into Indiana, they'll likely never get captured."

Sarah was impressed with his reasoning. "Did you counsel every runaway on all of this?"

"Yes, at every station on the railroad. They probably recite it in their sleep. Sadly, some of them don't have the energy to keep running far enough to elude the bounty hunters, and they are captured. For those poor souls, if they thought slavery was bad before they ran away, they soon learn that it's even worse afterward."

Sarah shuddered at the thought of what captured runaway slaves might endure. "So, in answer to Samuel's question?"

"Ah, yes. I figure I can probably get away with hiding out here another day or two at most. Everyone knows how close we are, Samuel. Eventually, they will come to question you, particularly after they search the ashes and find no bodies there. When I do resurface, I suggest our story goes something like this: I had had a terrible shock after being burned trying to save my ancestral home. The fire was an unfortunate accident caused by an oil lamp turning over. After wandering the countryside in a state of complete disorientation, I appeared at your door in the dead of night. You welcomed me like some scorched prodigal son, and next morning announced to the community that I'd miraculously survived, saints be praised!"

Samuel laughed. "Jews don't believe in saints, Benjamin. You're going to have to change that part."

"Anyway, you get the drift. The timing is the trickiest part. I can't wait too long or they'll sift through the ruins, and may find evidence of the tunnel. I'm counting on the assumption that the support beams came down in the blaze, and any sign of the tunnel is now gone. However, I'll feel better when I can get to the site myself and make sure of it. As soon as we get word that these last escapees are as far away as possible, I'll reappear, take charge of the cleanup, and run off anyone who asks too many questions. The sheriff isn't going to tell the truth, that's for sure. He's already lied to cover up his activities the other night. How is it going to look if he changes his story once I resurface? 'Oh, by the way, I forgot. Booth burned down his own house to drive me and my drunken friends away.' He'd be the laughingstock of the whole region."

"He already is," Samuel said.

Sarah wasn't so sure. "What if he does recant?"

"I've already thought of that. Then I say I set the fire because I was still in shock over the loss of my wife, and the horrific accident that killed her. Friends will attest that I've not been myself for some time, that I've been moody and difficult."

"That part will be easy. I volunteer," Samuel chirped and the squire glowered at him in mock irritation.

Sarah was relieved. "It certainly does sound plausible, and, despite Samuel's jokes, it's true. The last year truly has been terrible for you. I saw it in your face every day and felt awful for not being able to help."

"Ah, but you're wrong there. You did help, more than you'll ever know. Even before you healed Benjie, and before I . . . well, before we became . . . *friends*, it felt so good to have a woman in the house again, other than the servants, that is. You could talk about books, politics, art, and music—why, almost anything, now that I think about it. Exactly like Eleanor . . ."

He paused—as if it had occurred to him again how similar the two women were—then continued.

"I love my people, certainly, and Jesse especially has an exceptional mind. Only, I can't talk with them like I talk with you. So, I felt less lonely and lost, almost from the moment you walked in the door."

She was touched but also piqued once more by his avoidance of the word *slaves*. In light of their newfound intimacy, she hoped she could risk pursuing the matter further. The last time, over dinner with Samuel last spring, had been a disaster. However, a lot had changed since then.

"Sir, uh, Benjamin, I have to ask again, why do you never refer to your 'people' as slaves?"

"Because they're not slaves. They're all free—have been since shortly after my father's death."

She could have been knocked down with the proverbial feather. Her shocked expression was equaled only by that of Samuel.

"What?" they exclaimed in unison, and he chuckled.

"I wish I had a mirror right now so I could show you two how funny you look."

"Whatever for?" Sarah asked. "Why foster such a lie? What possible reason could there be?"

"Plenty, rest assured. Abolitionists are unpopular in these parts. Some are even murdered or at the very least, beaten, whipped, or tarred and feathered. I had to pretend to be a committed slaveholder."

Samuel wasn't convinced. "You're not afraid of anything. Why not stand up for what you believe, and come out with the truth?" Then he blushed, glanced at Sarah, and looked away. She knew what he was thinking. He was in love with Benjamin, and wasn't coming out with that truth, either.

"You're only partially right," the squire replied. "I'm afraid of many things, although, it's true, not a bunch of hooligans. One of my biggest fears was that the station I ran would be found out and shut down. I wanted to help as many slaves as possible for as long as possible. And we've had a good go at it. Annie keeps a count somewhere, and it's up to several hundred now."

Sarah was amazed. "How did you ever keep such a big operation secret?"

"Well, in truth, that was the hardest part. We had to keep

most of the workers in the dark. We simply couldn't trust them with the secret. Only Annie, Zeke, and Jesse were in on it, and I'd trust them with my life. To keep the others off our scent, we spread rumors about the hall and certain other places on the grounds, like the ferry landing, being haunted. That's all it took to keep the others away. As for the community, I became a member of every civic group I had time for, including some incendiary states' rights organizations. Those were hard meetings to stomach, I have to admit, yet I had to go along with them, to protect what we had going on here. And it all worked out for the best. Ask any slaveholder in the region what he thinks of Squire Benjamin Booth, and I guarantee he'll tell you I'm a fine fellow."

Samuel shook his head with an appreciative smile. "Sometimes you astound me, Benjamin. Now that we're hearing 'the whole truth and nothing but the truth,' what actually happened the night that I was shot?"

"I was wondering when you'd get to that. I had indeed visited the stables to check on my mare that night but only briefly as a ruse. It wasn't a difficult foaling at all, and Jesse had things well in hand. A group of runaways was down at the river waiting to be ferried across and I hurried down there to see that things went smoothly."

Samuel nodded. "That must have been when I saw you and tried to catch up with you."

"Exactly. However, on my way, I heard the sheriff and his men coming across the fields. I raced to the river and hid all the folks there inside the mouth of the tunnel, then covered it with brush. I was heading back across the fields to the hall when I saw you trying to elude the sheriff and heard his shot ring out. I beat them to you, slung you over my shoulder, and raced back to the house faster than I ever would have thought possible carrying a dead weight like that."

Samuel's eyes filled. "And I would have indeed been dead without you."

He got up, a little sadly, Sarah thought. "Benjie, would you like to go with Uncle Samuel to his tannery and see how the men make leather?"

The boy deserted the puppies in an instant. "Oh, Papa, can I, please?"

"Of course, son."

They all exchanged hugs before Samuel and Benjie made their exit. Sarah had never seen the two men hug; however, they did now—a little cautiously because of the squire's burns—and she got the distinct feeling that neither one of them wanted the embrace to end. When it did, they looked at each other with silly grins, then became self-conscious and made rude jibes to cover their feelings.

When the others had gone, Sarah realized that she and the squire were alone together for the first time in a long while, and certainly for the first time since they had begun to address each other with first names. A prickle of anxiety made her face flush, and she looked down, pretending to find a pattern in the tablecloth fascinating. He surprised her, as he was so prone to do, especially lately.

"I've a mind to take a walk. Will you join me?"

"You can't. You're in hiding."

"Be thankful for stubborn women," he quipped, and they both laughed. "I'll put on a wide-brimmed hat and muffler, and no one will know me. Come, now. Walk with me."

She helped him navigate the path from the breakfast room to

the cloakroom off the foyer. She winced along with him when his movements irritated his burns. Finally, they had him garbed in a suitable disguise and ventured out onto the bustling city streets.

Having spent most of the last six months in the country—save for one glittering night at the Galt House Hotel—Sarah found all the activity a bit overwhelming. Everywhere she looked, people scurried about, trying to get somewhere, and every single one of them seemed to be in a hurry. Carriages and wagons vied for space on the narrow, muddy streets, and vendors of all sorts hawked their wares. It was all exactly as it had been the day she arrived in Louisville, a day that now seemed to her a million years ago.

He surprised her again by taking her arm and putting it in his. "It's a busy place, isn't it?"

She nodded. "That's exactly what I said to Jesse the day he picked me up on the levee last spring."

"Would you miss it?"

She studied him, trying to figure out what was in his head. "Why do you ask?"

He gave her another one of his enigmatic smiles. "Did I ever tell you that I have property in California?"

She wanted to scream, "*Of course not*, you maddening creature! You keep everything secret, or lie to cover the truth." However, she simply smiled and said, no, she didn't think so.

"Well, I do, and I've been thinking about going out there to develop it. I believe the soil and climate would make an outstanding vineyard, and I'd like to open a winery one day."

"Why? This is your home. You're loved and respected here."

"For now, yes, but not when the truth gets out, and it will eventually. The truth always does."

Sarah thought about Samuel's secret and hoped the squire was wrong. The tenderhearted scholar would never survive the hatred heaped on him if his true nature was revealed.

"Besides, my work here is done. I believe we've helped as many people cross over as we're ever going to. The vigilantes are becoming more aggressive all the time. Why, look at how the sheriff behaved the other day. What effrontery! I'm a leading citizen here, and he dared to take me on like that with a bunch of thugs in league to boot. We won the day, but that's still a very bad sign for me. War is coming any time, and I'd like to get Benjie as far away from it as possible. He's seen enough horror in his short life."

He stopped and turned to face her. "And you. I'd like to get you as far away from it as possible as well. It seems your life has hardly been a picnic, either."

She couldn't meet the intensity in his eyes. "Well, thank you for worrying about me. I will still need work, after all, and, and . . ." She trailed off and looked away.

Risking another breach of etiquette by touching her face in public, he took her chin in his hand and lifted it so she could meet his gaze. "I'm not asking you to come with me as Benjie's governess. Have I been foolish and wrongly assumed that you might have some . . . feelings for me?"

The dam in her heart broke and she leapt into his arms, burrowing deep into his big, barrel chest.

"No, no, of course not! I do! I do!" Then she remembered his burns and pulled away. "Oh, dear, your burns. I'm so sorry. Did I hurt you?"

He winced a bit, but pulled her back into his arms, and sighed with contentment. "My dear, I'm so glad to have you in my embrace at last, nothing else matters but that. After my poor efforts at flirting last spring failed so miserably, I assumed this moment would never be. I even tried to pair you off with Samuel, who was closer to your age. Thank God that didn't work."

Out of the corner of her eye, she noticed the disapproving stares their open displays of affection were attracting from passersby, but she didn't care.

She looked up at him and they melted even closer together. They stood that way for a long time while the noise of the city faded away. Eventually, a group of schoolboys began to point and giggle at them. They disengaged reluctantly, but continued hand in hand, walking down the sidewalks of Market Street, and into a new life together.

THE END

EPILOGUE

I grew up in the 1950s in the suburbs of Louisville, Kentucky, where life seemed very quiet and unremarkable. As a result, I was excited to learn in grade school history lessons that Louisville had a remarkable past, including playing a strategic role as an important hub in the Underground Railroad.

As a border state, Kentucky and one of its northernmost cities, Louisville, were the perfect locations for "conductors" to help runaway slaves cross into the free state of Indiana, usually at New Albany. There, a number of ministers offered their parsonages, and other abolitionists offered their homes as shelters for the runaways until their passage farther north could be arranged.

Researching this history further, I was proud to learn that Louisville and New Albany had been some of the railroad's busiest sites. Because these operations were clandestine, records were secret and firm figures are hard to find today. However, estimates are that over the years that the railroad operated, hundreds and possibly even thousands of escaped slaves passed through railroad shelters in Louisville to find freedom in Indiana and beyond.

When writing became a passion for me in my teens and twenties, I hoped to one day write a historical novel set in Louisville, with the Underground Railroad as its backdrop. As a lover of gothic romances, most notably the genre's prototypes, *Jane Eyre*, *Northanger Abbey*, and *Rebecca*, I envisioned a suspenseful tale along the lines of those works. In it, the *de rigueur* plain, spinster governess would fall in love with the mysterious, older plantation owner as unsettling events— apparent hauntings, and other "things that go bump in the night"—unfolded around her. As the plot thickened, she would find that things were not as they appeared to be—a trademark of the genre. When the denouement came, she would find that the plantation owner's particular mystery was that he was a conductor for the Underground Railroad, and his operation was one of the busiest ones in the South.

I started writing this tale while I was in undergraduate studies more than forty years ago. However, life, in the form of having babies, earning degrees and pursuing careers, got in the way. That manuscript disappeared long ago, somewhere between baby number one, baby number two, and a second or third change of homes. Three years ago, forced retirement for health reasons brought the mixed blessing of expanded opportunities for writing. Since then, I have written three books and published two of them.

For this latest work, the mere finishing of it has been a special labor of love for me. Getting to tie up forty-year-old "loose ends" has special meaning for us when we're moving into our "golden years." I hope it will find its way into the hands of readers, one way or another, and that whoever does come across it will enjoy reading it as much as I have enjoyed writing it.

—Fred Schloemer

HISTORICAL NOTES

Writing a period piece about a time in American history when slavery, racism, and racist language were the norms is fraught with special challenges and risks. That has been the case with this project.

Some of my dilemmas have centered on the matter of how to use language that was historically accurate to the time while still being sensitive to modern-day racial sensibilities. For instance, I use the now outdated and some would even say offensive term *Negro* to describe the slave characters in my story. I do so because in 1860 America, the terms African American, and black simply didn't exist.

On the other hand, I specifically avoid some other labels and terminology that were common to the time, such as "darkie," because it is clearly racist by the standards of any era. Similarly, I avoided writing the African American characters' dialogue in dialect, which is usually offensive, although the matriarch Annie, who came from Africa, and the elder Kplorm, do speak more colloquially than their children who were born in America.

Through these efforts, I hope that I have managed to walk the line between historical accuracy and modern-day political correctness. It is my further hope that nothing in these pages gives offense to anyone of any race.

In another vein, I struggled with plausibility issues as I strove to weave historical events into a suspenseful, fictional tale featuring apparent hauntings and other mysterious happenings. Along the way, I learned that this is probably one of the most difficult tasks for any historical fiction writer. The irony of it is that sometimes the "made-up" aspects of the tale seem more plausible than the factual ones.

For example, the plantation featured in this story is modeled after Riverside, the classically beautiful Georgian home at Farnsley-Moreman Landing southwest of Louisville. It was built in 1838 and operated as a productive plantation at the time this tale takes place, although it was empty because it was between owners in the 1850s. Riverside was also a busy riverboat stopover, where travelers could buy food prepared at the house and take a respite from their journeys. A family-owned ferry operated there as well, and goods unloaded from the riverboats were ferried across the river to Indiana for distribution and sale, or carted elsewhere into Kentucky.

As for the real nature of the Underground Railroad, we now know that the way it truly worked has been obfuscated through the years by revisionist historians, much like many other things in American history. (See References for sources). From the Civil War well into the twentieth century, the widely accepted narrative was that white abolitionists ran the operation. In fact, it was primarily freed African Americans who faced grave risks to foray back into slave territory and guide runaways to safety and freedom.

Another spurious aspect of the traditional story is that the railroad used an extensive network of cellars and tunnels where runaways would hide and move unseen from station to station.

Such cellars and tunnels did exist, but they were not as widely used as they have been made out to be. In reality, most runaways were moved from place to place not through tunnels, but by hiding among goods being transported from slave to non-slave states, in wagons, boats, trains, or ferries. Despite these facts, I have included a tunnel in this story, because, after all, they're so "creepy" and I wanted to include that element in my own gothic-inspired romance.

The Underground Railroad has been called the first civil rights movement in American history. As with any movement, it required the coordinated planning and actions of many players of various races, roles, and socioeconomic groups. African Americans couldn't have done it without the aid of white supporters, and white supporters couldn't have done it without the aid of freed slaves. Most abolitionists weren't wealthy people, so they couldn't have done what they did without funding by white sympathizers who were affluent. Still, freed African Americans deserve the lion's share of credit for making the Underground Railroad work so well for so long, and history owes them an apology for minimizing their importance.

In light of these facts, I have made my story one that shows the essential role of the African American characters in the overall operation of an Underground Railroad station on a fictional plantation. There may be a white master who appears to be directing things, but as the plot unfolds, we find that is not necessarily the full truth.

Finally, the part of this story in which quilts are hung out to relay coded messages and directions to runaways is based on longstanding historical accounts, although the accuracy of these accounts is currently under dispute by most modern historians.

I have nonetheless included that element in my story because I feel that it adds to the mystery and suspense of the tale.

I need to make one last clarification. The owners of Riverside were never reputed to be involved in the Underground Railroad. However, if they had wished to be, their home and ferry would have been the perfect places to do so. Indeed, many of the actual sites where runaways did cross the river to Indiana were in the vicinity of Farnsley-Moreman Landing.

I've come to believe that the theatrical device of asking viewers (or in this case, readers) to suspend their disbelief is an important aid in the writing of historical fiction, mysteries, and romances. Using that device, I hope I have managed to craft a tale which, while largely imaginative and fanciful, is also believable.

However, if any reader finds plausibility strained anywhere in these pages, I would ask them to enter into the spirit of playfulness, which is an essential part of reading mystery and romance. For when all is said and done, it's a tale that celebrates life, kinship, and love—but most of all freedom.

—F. S.

REFERENCES

Burns, Eleanor, and Sue Bouchard. *Underground Railroad Sampler*. San Marcos, CA: Quilts in a Day Publishing, 2003.

Hudson, Dr. J. Blaine. "Crossing the 'Dark Line': Fugitive Slaves and the Underground Railroad in Louisville and North Central Kentucky" (excerpt). *Kentucky's Underground Railroad: Passage to Freedom*. Lexington, KY: Kentucky Educational Television. http://www.ket.org/underground/research/crossing.htm

"Quilts of the Underground Railroad." Wikipedia, https://en.wikipedia.org/wiki/Quilts_of_the_Underground_Railroad.

Rosen, Marty. "Louisville's Little-Known Connection to the Underground Railroad [Communities]," Louisville.com website, https://www.louisville.com/content/louisvilles-little-known-connection-underground-railroad-communities.

ABOUT THE AUTHOR

Fred Schloemer, Ed.D., is a career psychotherapist, author, and educator based in Louisville, Kentucky. He has published widely in professional journals and regional newspapers, and has authored several self-help books. However, his first love is writing fiction.

He has previously published four books. *Just One More Bird* is a self-help book for small children of alcoholics. *From a Land in Between* is an anthology of short stories and poems dealing with sexual diversity. *Parenting Adult Children: Real Stories of Families Turning Challenges into Successes* won the 2012 Nautilus Book Awards Silver Certificate for books that promote positive social change. *Behind the Footlights* is a novel that pays tribute to community theater; *LEO* magazine named it one of its 2015 top ten "must-read" books by Kentucky authors.

This latest work is his first romance and was more than forty years in the making. He now lives in semi-retirement with his husband, Ernie Schnell, an oncology nurse, on their small horse farm in southern Indiana. He invites readers and others to contact him at FredSchloemer63@gmail.com.